My Epic Fairy Tale FAIL

ANNA STANISZEWSKI

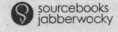

sourcebooks
jabberwocky

Published by Jabberwocky, an imprint of Sourcebooks, Inc.
P.O. Box 4410, Naperville, Illinois 60567-4410
(630) 961-3900
Fax: (630) 961-2168
www.jabberwockykids.com

Library of Congress Cataloging-in-Publication data is on file with the publisher.

Source of Production: Webcom, Toronto, Canada
Date of Production: January 2013
Run Number: 19467

Printed and bound in Canada.
WC 10 9 8 7 6 5 4 3 2 1

This book belongs to*:

_____

*Disclaimer: By printing your name above, you hereby agree to become an Adventurer for life and vow to help *all* creatures of the magical variety (including angry, smelly mermaids).** Failure to carry out your duties will result in a disciplinary hearing before the Committee. Do *not* bring a cell phone. They hate cell phones.

**We are not responsible for injuries sustained on missions. Avoid trolls, sea monsters, unicorns, pitchfork-wielding villagers, wolves in workout gear, giant b—Well, you get the picture.

"The universe is made of stories, not of atoms."

—Muriel Rukeyser

PART I

Chapter One

If someone tells you that you're being sent to a magical mermaid land, take my advice and spend the day at the aquarium instead. Then you can have a nice lunch, feed some dolphins, and not get caught in the middle of a mer-people war.

Mermaids are nothing like the gorgeous girls you see in movies. In reality, they're bitter creatures who hate the water because it turns their skin pruney. Even though their tails don't transform into legs, that doesn't stop them from desperately wanting to live on land so they can spend their days basking in the sun. Which is why the Green Tails and the Blue Tails were fighting over an island the size of a school bus. And why I, Jenny the Adventurer, had been sent to stop them.

To be honest, I wasn't doing a very good job so far. If I'd been on this mission alone, things probably would have been fine. But my bosses—the all-powerful and all-annoying Committee—didn't trust me after I'd threatened to quit being an adventurer, so they'd found me a baby-sitter: Jasmine, the wimpiest girl in the universe.

"Jenny," she said as the two of us huddled behind a sand dune. The mermaid armies were lined up on the beach, on opposite sides of the tiny island, balanced on their tails like trained seals. "I think our current position is overly exposed. Maybe we should relocate?"

We *were* right in between the two merpeople clans, but since the island only had three sand dunes and one puny palm tree, there was nowhere else for us to go.

"Relocate to where?" I made sure to keep my nose covered with my T-shirt as I spoke. Fun fact about mermaids: they smell like a bucket of old fish.

Before Jasmine could answer, a shout rang out among the Blue Tails: "Load the catapult!"

A second later, a bunch of sea sponges shot through the air.

Jasmine shrieked and covered her head. "I think this situation is getting too dangerous! We should call for our guides."

I stared at her. Jasmine was only a couple years older

than me, but she acted like a little old lady. Was she really afraid of some flying sponges? "Jasmine, we only just got here. And we can't abandon an assignment."

"Spray!" one of the Green Tails yelled. A shower of starfish sailed over our heads.

"There's no shame in walking away from an adventure and trying again another day," said Jasmine. "Better safe than sorry." We adventurers sure love our cheesy sayings.

I guess I couldn't blame Jasmine for being so cautious. Thanks to Klarr, the evil clown sorcerer, she'd spent days as a bear statue. Even now, weeks after I'd managed to defeat the crazy clown, Jasmine claimed that dust came out of her nose whenever she sneezed.

"We can figure this out," I said over the dolphin-like war cries of the nearby clan. "Where there's a will, there's a way, right?"

Jasmine's dark eyes narrowed. "Are you sure you're not putting us in unnecessary danger so you'll have a better story to share with your friends?"

I almost laughed thinking of how Trish and Melissa, my regular-life friends, would react when I told them what merpeople were really like. My friends couldn't get enough of hearing about my adventures. Trish was even doing a huge English paper on magic, which meant she asked me about a hundred questions a day.

"Reload the catapult!" Something flew past that looked suspiciously like a flailing octopus. Okay, this was getting ridiculous.

"I have an idea." I pulled off my sock and poured a handful of sand into it. Hey, if my plan failed, I could always stun the merpeople with foot odor.

"What are you doing?" said Jasmine, staring at me in horror. "You might get some type of foot fungus in a place like this!"

I resisted the urge to smack her with my sock. Instead, I jumped up and yelled, "Fish! Get your delicious fish! Whoever stops fighting first gets this super-amazing, tasty treat." I waved my sock around like there was a fishy delicacy inside.

The fighting stopped and all mermaid eyes swung toward me. I couldn't help smiling. Finally, I'd gotten their attention.

"What kind of fish?" one of the Blue Tails asked, sniffing the air.

"Not so fast." I hid the sock behind my back. "First, we need to get you guys to stop fighting. Let's sit down—er, I mean, float around, and talk about this. There has to be a way to work things out."

"The only way is for the Green Tails to leave our land!" cried one of the mermaids.

"*Your* land?" demanded a blue-tailed merman as he shimmied forward, snake-like. "We saw it first."

"Prove it, tuna breath!"

"No, *you* prove it, shark face!"

A chorus of chirps and clicks erupted, followed by sea-lion-like howls.

"Hey!" I yelled, swinging my sock over my head, but no one was listening to me anymore. Soon rocks and seaweed and shellfish were flying through the air again. I managed to duck to avoid getting hit in the eye with an oyster.

"*Now* can we go?" said Jasmine.

I opened my mouth to tell her we weren't going anywhere until we figured out a way to settle this mess, but I was interrupted by a loud *Pop*! I turned just as my magical guide, Anthony the Gnome, materialized next to me.

"Hey there, Jenny-girl!" he said. "I have great news!"

"You know a way to stop these crazies from battling each other?" I said, emptying my sandy sock and pulling it back on. I really hoped Jasmine was wrong about the dangers of foot fungus.

Anthony's smile faltered. "Oh. No, I have no idea how to fix that. It's probably hopeless. In fact, you're both being taken off this assignment."

"What? Says who?" I asked, just as Jasmine let out a loud sigh of relief beside me.

"Says the Committee," said Anthony, tugging on his bright orange beard. "This mission is being put on hold."

That was weird. The Committee never let adventurers give up on missions. It was in our contract. "Why? What's going on?" I asked.

"Well—" Anthony began.

A broken oar sliced into the sand next to me like a javelin, causing Jasmine to let out an I'm-being-murdered scream.

"On second thought," I said, "Anthony, how about taking us back to my house before you tell me about it?"

The merpeople sounded deafening battle cries and started furiously slithering toward each other. Apparently, they were done throwing things. Now it was time for hair-pulling and tail-slapping. There was no way Jasmine could handle that without having a total meltdown.

"Anthony!" I said. "Get us out of here!"

He harrumphed to himself. "Always being ordered around," he said. "That's the life of a gnome." Then he snapped his fingers, and with a *Pop!*, we were out of there.

Chapter Two

After some mind-numbing spinning between the mermaid world and good old Earth, the three of us landed on my bedroom carpet. I groaned and pulled some seaweed out of my hair.

"Thank you, Anthony," said Jasmine, brushing sand off her khakis. "That was getting exceptionally unsafe."

"No problem-o," said the gnome, snapping his fingers again. I expected a candy bar to materialize in his hands, so I nearly fell over in shock when a stalk of celery appeared instead.

Anthony saw me staring, and he made a sour face. "Dr. Bradley put me on a diet. I can't conjure anything but health food now."

"Wow." After all the adventures I'd been on, it took a lot to surprise me, but Anthony on a diet was about the strangest thing I could imagine. "So what's the big news?"

Anthony glanced at Jasmine. "It's kind of private. And Dr. Bradley made me swear not to tell you unless he was there too."

Now that was interesting. What could be so important?

Jasmine took the hint. "If I'm not needed anymore, I'm off to crochet some orange elephant earrings. Jenny, I can make you a pair if you'd like."

I smiled weakly, fingering the hideous frog earrings she'd given me for my thirteenth birthday last week. They were supposed to remind me of Crong and Ribba, talking frogs from one of my previous adventures, but mostly they just made me feel a little creepy crawly. Still, it was nice of her to offer. "Um, sure. Thanks."

"Wait," said Anthony as Jasmine headed for the door. "The Committee members sent word that they want to see you."

Her eyes widened. "I thought the Committee never sees anyone."

"Not usually," he said, "but that's the message I got."

"Whatever you do," I told her, "make sure to turn off your cell phone. The Committee members are pretty psycho about that kind of thing."

Jasmine straightened her blouse and smoothed back her

hair. For some reason, she always dressed like a banker. "See you next time!" she said. Then she nodded at Anthony, who snapped his fingers to send her off to the Committee. Instantly, she was gone.

I went to pull off the small bag that was slung over my shoulder—the "adventuring kit" I'd started bringing along on missions—but Anthony stopped me. "You might need that," he said.

As I adjusted the strap of my bag, I expected Anthony to pop us over to Dr. Bradley's house, even though he lived just around the corner. But the gnome headed for the door instead, grumbling something about needing to get more exercise.

On the way out of the house, we passed by my aunt in the kitchen. She was in the middle of an art therapy session with a raccoon patient. They were both painting pictures of fruit, though the raccoon's bowl of apples looked a lot more lifelike than my aunt's basket of bananas.

"Hi, Aunt Evie!" I called.

"Hello, dear," she called back, waving her paintbrush. She didn't seem to notice the brightly colored gnome walking alongside me, which was a good thing since my aunt had no idea about the adventuring part of my life. As far as she knew, I was a totally normal kid, and my parents had been totally normal dentists. Sometimes having a scatterbrained animal psychotherapist for a guardian had its advantages.

"Bye, Aunt Evie!" I said, opening the front door.

"Bye, dear!" she called after me while the raccoon chirped in my general direction.

When we were outside, Anthony conjured up a head of lettuce and started crunching away with a disgusted look on his face. He reminded me of a disgruntled hamster.

"How long is this diet supposed to last?" I asked.

"Too long," Anthony muttered. "My high-school reunion is coming up next week, and I want to look great." He grabbed his round belly and gave it a jiggle.

"Wait. You went to high school? Like a gnome one?"

"Yes, indeed," he said. "And I was popular too. Played football and soccer and cottonball."

I didn't bother asking what cottonball was. The thought of teams of gnomes playing sports against each other was plenty entertaining.

"So am I being sent on another mission?" I asked. Dr. Bradley had helped me work out a deal with the Committee so I would only be sent on one magical assignment a month until I was done with school. That meant more time for friends, family, and unfortunately, homework. But maybe something serious was happening in the magical worlds that meant I had to be sent off on an adventure again.

"I can't say," said the gnome. *Crunch. Crunch. Crunch.* Eating healthy sure was loud.

"Well, do you at least have any idea how long it will take?" I knew Anthony would laugh at me if I told him this, but I really wanted to go to a dance at school this weekend. Actually, it would be my first dance *ever*. Trish and Melissa had promised we'd all go together.

Anthony shook his head. "I'll let the doctor explain."

Dr. Bradley no longer lived on my street, but he'd found a new place that was also in my neighborhood. It was a tiny house from the outside, but Dr. Bradley had worked some of his magic to make all his things—including his giant library—fit inside.

Not surprisingly, we found Dr. Bradley in his junk room happily sifting through a box of old toasters. If anyone ever made a TV show about magical hoarders, he'd be the star.

"Aren't these incredible?" he said, flashing a toothy grin.

"They look broken," I pointed out. One of them was so burned that it was just a black lump.

"They're broken *now*," said Dr. Bradley. "But there was a time when they worked swimmingly. I think I'd like to honor their service by putting them in a display case."

I had to choke down a laugh as I imagined the toaster display next to the other cases the doctor had set up, including one filled with creepy headless dolls. Dr. Bradley was well on his way to having the most disturbing museum ever.

"You have news for me?" I said.

"Ah, yes." Dr. Bradley grabbed his cane and got to his feet. "Anthony and I have something very exciting to tell you. You're being sent on another mission!"

"*That's* the big news? I thought there was some kind of adventuring emergency going on."

"It's not just any old mission, Jenny-girl," said Anthony, popping some grapes in his mouth. "You're being sent to the Land of Tales."

The room spun around me for a second. "The Land of Tales? You mean the place…?"

"Where your parents were last seen," said Dr. Bradley, nodding with his whole body. "I specifically requested that you be sent on any missions that opened up there, but since the land has been closed off from the outside world, there haven't been any in years. Imagine my delight this morning when I received a message that Princess Nartha had requested help from the Committee."

I couldn't believe it. This was the moment I'd been waiting for practically my whole life! Finally, after nothing but dead ends, I'd have a chance to get more clues about my parents' disappearance. I'd tried to find out information from Aunt Evie, but she always got teary-eyed and said the past was too painful to stir up.

I glanced at the bracelet around my wrist, which had once belonged to my mother. I could almost hear its purple gems whispering to me. *Find your parents, Jenny. They're waiting for you.*

Okay, so missing my parents was possibly making me a little crazy. But I didn't just miss them; I felt like my whole body was bursting with questions about them. Where were they? Were they still alive? And what could I do to get them back?

"Wait," I said. "Jasmine isn't coming with me, is she?" Jasmine was nice enough, and if I'd met her at school, the two of us might have even been friends. But if I had to go on another adventure with her and her weird yarn jewelry—especially an adventure this important—I didn't think I could keep from strangling her. Or at least throwing a sea sponge at her.

"No," said Dr. Bradley. "The Committee has agreed to let you handle this one on your own."

"Good. So when do we leave?" I didn't even care about the school dance anymore. There'd be other dances, but I only had one set of parents.

"First, I must brief you on the mission," said Dr. Bradley, pushing his glasses up his long nose. He hobbled over to an armchair and settled into it, like he was getting ready for story time.

"Can't Anthony tell me everything once we get there? I don't think I can wait another minute." I'd never been so eager to go on an assignment in my life.

Dr. Bradley glanced at Anthony, and the two of them had a silent conversation, nodding and blinking and nodding again.

"Is there a problem?" I asked. "Are you guys having some sort of episode?"

"No, no," the doctor said finally. "I suppose it would be all right if Anthony briefed you. But be careful, Jenny. We've heard very little about what's been happening in the

Land of Tales since your parents disappeared there. You never know—"

"Don't worry about me."

"It's just, the Committee is concerned that..." Dr. Bradley's words faded away, and he looked suddenly interested in some invisible lint on his sweater vest.

"The Committee members don't think I should go, do they?"

"They're just worried, Jenny-girl," said Anthony. "They think it's dangerous."

I shook my head. "That's not it. They don't think I can do it." That's why they'd had Jasmine babysitting me, to make sure I was following all their rules and being a good little adventurer. It stung that the Committee members didn't have faith in me, especially after I'd been going on mission after mission for them for over three years. If anyone should have a chance to go to the world where my parents had vanished, it was me.

"Come on, Anthony," I said. "We're going."

"But, Jenny," said Dr. Bradley, "there are some things you should know before—"

"I'll be fine. I promise." I shot Anthony an insistent look. He sighed and nodded.

My Epic Fairy Tale Fail

There was a loud *Pop*! and Dr. Bradley's house faded away, replaced by a blinding mix of colors. Normally, I dreaded traveling in between worlds, but this time I barely even noticed it. All I could think about was that after all these years, I might finally get some answers.

Chapter Three

When I opened my eyes, I expected to find myself in a magical kingdom. So I couldn't figure out why we were outside Aunt Evie's house again, standing in her flower beds.

"Anthony?" I said, brushing mulch off my sneakers. "Did you miscalculate or something?"

He grinned. "Just a slight detour to pick up a couple of passengers." He plucked a marigold and popped it in his mouth.

"Passengers?" I echoed just as someone came out from behind the bushes. Technically, two someones. A tall girl with long, straight hair, and a shorter, rounder girl with bright purple glasses. "Melissa? Trish? What are you guys doing here?"

"We're coming with you!" Melissa cried, her hair swirling around her shoulders. "Isn't that fantabulous?"

"This is finally our chance to see what you do," said

Trish. She seal-clapped with excitement, reminding me way too much of a crazed mermaid.

I glared at Anthony. "What's going on?"

"I figured it couldn't hurt," he said, not meeting my eyes. "It's only a tiny mission, and they were very convincing."

"Are you crazy? What about the Committee? Those old women will totally flip if they find out you brought regular humans to a magical world!" The Committee loved wiping people's minds if they knew too much about magic. I couldn't let that happen to my friends. Not again.

Anthony shook his head. "The Committee members will never know unless we tell them." He turned to Trish and Melissa. "So, do you have my payment?"

My mouth dropped open. "You guys bribed him?"

"It was Trish's idea!" said Melissa.

Trish pushed up her glasses as a mischievous smile spread across her face. She unzipped her backpack and took out an enormous package of candy hearts. "Actually," she said, "I got the idea from you, Jenny. Remember when you told me Anthony would do anything for some candy? It turns out that's true."

The gnome's already-red cheeks turned even redder. "What can I say, Jenny-girl? I couldn't go another day eating nothing but rabbit food. One small bag of candy won't hurt, right?"

"Sorry, guys," I said. "You can't come with me."

Trish's face fell. "But, Jenny, my English paper will be so much better if I can see a magical place for myself. And Mrs. Brown said there's a contest I can send my paper to. I would give anything to win."

She did have a point. Writing about magic would be a whole lot easier if you'd actually seen it in action. And winning an essay contest would go a long way in helping Trish stand out from her four brothers and sisters. She'd never admit it, but I knew Trish was always trying to get her parents to notice her.

"Please, Jenny?" said Melissa, her eyes big and round like a cartoon character's. "Think of all the songs I'll be able to write about fairies and dragons." She waggled her eyebrows. "And about cute princes."

Unlike Trish, Melissa was an only child, but since her father was an opera singer and her mother was a country star, Melissa was always trying to prove to her parents that she'd inherited their music genes. I knew she dreamed of writing the perfect hit song. Maybe traveling to another world would give her more exciting things to sing about.

No, I told myself. Just because my friends desperately wanted to come with me didn't mean I should put them in harm's way.

"My missions aren't like that," I said. "I've never even met a fairy. Dragons will just try to barbecue you. And princes are more trouble than they're worth, no matter how cute they are." I could tell my friends weren't buying it. "I'm serious, guys. My adventures are nothing like Disney movies. They can be really dangerous."

"Oh, your friends will be fine," Anthony said with a wave of his plump hand. "You always manage to come out alive, don't you?"

"Barely," I muttered. I turned back to Melissa and Trish. "If anything happened to you guys—"

"It won't," said Trish. "We'll be careful. See?" She pulled a purple bike helmet out of her bag and plopped it on her head.

"Super-uber careful," Melissa added, putting on a neon hockey mask. I had to bite my lip to keep from laughing.

"You won't have to worry about us. We're prepared for anything," said Trish. She held up a thick book of fairy tales. "I'm like a walking encyclopedia!"

"And," Melissa chimed in, "I've been eating fortune cookies for weeks and saving all the little messages. We'll have tons of cheesy sayings to get us through the adventure." She reached in her pants pocket and pulled out a fortune. Her eyes widened as she read it, and she let out a little squeal.

"What does it say?" said Trish.

"It says: 'A thrilling time is in your future.'" Melissa crossed her arms in front of her chest, a smug look on her face. "See?"

"It doesn't get any clearer than that," said Anthony. "You have to bring them with you, Jenny-girl. The cookie gods demand it."

"But what about the dance tomorrow night? We'll probably miss it," I said, knowing I sounded a little desperate. "It's the last one of the year. Weren't you guys excited about going?"

Trish let out a sputtering laugh. "Are you kidding? Who cares about a dance when this is going to be so much better?"

"Puh-lease?" said Melissa, looking like she might get on her knees and beg.

What could I say? Bringing them on my adventure was probably a terrible idea, but my friends obviously weren't going to take no for an answer. Maybe having them along wouldn't be so bad. Then they'd finally understand that my job wasn't as easy as they were always making it out to be. Besides, having Melissa and Trish with me could make things a lot more fun.

"Okay, fine," I said.

Melissa shrieked and jumped up and down while Trish held up her arms in a touchdown pose.

"But you have to listen to me, okay?" I went on. "If I tell you to run, you run. If I tell you to hide, you hide. If I tell you to pole-vault, you—"

"I think they get the picture, Jenny-girl." Anthony rolled his eyes. "Let's get going already!"

I sighed and nodded, hoping I wasn't making a huge mistake. Then I held on to Trish and Melissa, who were both bouncing around like bobblehead dolls, and—*Pop!*—we were off.

Chapter Four

When I opened my eyes again, we were in the middle of the most amazing meadow I'd ever seen. It felt like we'd been dropped right in the middle of Candyland. Lush grass surrounded us like a green carpet, basketball-sized flowers swayed in the breeze, and dozens of sparkling butterflies flitted through the air. Maybe I'd been wrong when I told Melissa and Trish that my adventures were nothing like Disney movies.

I heard my friends groaning beside me. They were both sprawled on the ground, looking almost as green as the grass.

"Welcome to the joys of inter-world travel," I said, helping them to their feet.

"Ugh, that felt like getting sucked through a straw or something," said Melissa, pulling off her hockey mask and rubbing her temples.

"Is it normal to feel like you don't have knees?" said Trish, adjusting her backpack.

"It'll wear off in a second." I motioned for them to look around. "I hope it was worth it."

My friends gasped in unison as they finally noticed our surroundings. Then Trish started spinning in happy circles like a character in a cheesy movie.

"It's goooorgeous!" Melissa belted out in her amazing singing voice.

"Welcome to the Land of Tales," said Anthony, sounding like a nasally tour guide. "On your left is a field. On your right is a rock. Through there"—he pointed toward a forest—"is the village and, beyond it, the palace where Princess Nartha is waiting for us."

"Why did you pop us in all the way out here, then?" I asked.

"It'll give me some time to fill you in," said Anthony, setting off toward the woods. "Plus, Dr. Bradley insists that the more I walk, the more calories I'll burn." He shook his head like that was the most ridiculous idea he'd ever heard. "The main thing you need to know about the Land of Tales is that it's the origin of all fairy tales."

"What do you mean?" I hurried to catch up while Trish

and Melissa trailed behind us, their eyes huge and their mouths hanging open.

"You know all those princess-needs-to-be-rescued stories?" said Anthony. "They all originated here. Every time a story has a babbling brook in it, this is where it came from."

"That makes sense," Trish chimed in. "No one knows the origin of fairy tales, but there are similar stories all over our world. It figures they'd all come from one place." She really did sound like an encyclopedia with legs.

"So why did Princess Nartha ask us for help?" I said as we came to an overgrown trail that cut through the woods.

"In a nutshell," said Anthony, "the land is under a curse that's draining all the magic. For years now, the magic has been getting weaker and weaker. Eventually, the whole land will be affected, including the field where we first popped in."

"What happens when there's no magic at all?" said Trish.

Anthony pointed to a stream flowing past us. "Remember how I mentioned a babbling brook? That's what it looks like now that the magic is almost gone." Instead of babbling, the brook was moaning and sighing like it was in pain. "Once the last of the magic disappears, the brook will just be an ordinary stream. It won't be able to say a word."

"Poor thing!" cried Melissa. She rushed over to the brook and ran her fingers over the top of the water, like she was trying to pet it. "It sounds so sad. Can't we do anything?"

"How long has this been going on?" I asked Anthony after I'd managed to get Melissa back on the path with us.

"From what Princess Nartha told us, the magic first started growing weaker seven years ago," said Anthony.

"Wait, seven years?" I felt a jolt in my stomach. "That's how long my parents have been gone. Do you think the two things could be related somehow?"

Anthony shook his head. "We were told a witch named Ilda is behind the curse. She's the only one in the land with her magic still intact, so she must be responsible. Somehow, she's found a way to slowly suck up the land's magic." He glanced at me with actual concern on his round face. "Watch out for Ilda, Jenny-girl. She's crazy with a capital Q."

"I'll be fine," I said. Since when did Dr. Bradley and Anthony worry about me so much? Normally, they seemed perfectly happy to send me off to face creatures that either wanted to eat me or to turn me into a pet. "Do you have any idea how I'm supposed to get the land's magic back?"

"According to Ilda, someone needs to complete her Three Impossible Tasks by the end of the seven years to restore the magic. Otherwise, it will be gone for good."

"Let me guess," I said. "The seven years are almost up?"

"Correct-o! You have three days left before the curse can't be reversed," said Anthony.

"Three days?" Did people think we adventurers *liked* having ticking clocks hanging over our heads? "Why didn't they ask the Committee for help right away?"

"Not everyone is a fan of the Committee and what it stands for." Anthony looked like he wanted to say more, but then he just shook his head and kept walking. He was rarely so quiet, but I figured that might just be a low-blood-sugar thing. I decided not to push him in case he was about to crack.

Instead, I listened to Trish and Melissa gushing about our surroundings. The Land of Tales might have been in trouble, but with its bright blue sky and chirping lollipop-colored birds, it was still straight out of a storybook. I almost expected rainbow bubbles to start floating down from the sky.

"I can't believe you get to visit places like this all the time!" said Melissa. She whistled along with the birds as they flitted past, trilling away.

"Trust me, they're not all like this." I started to tell my friends about how crazy Merland had been, even showing them a handful of smelly sand that was still in my pocket, but I could tell they didn't really believe me.

When we came to a dirt road, I heard something rumbling toward us. Whatever it was, it was moving *fast*. I just managed to yank my friends backward as two girls sprinted past us at full speed. Each girl was holding on to the handlebars of a bicycle as she ran.

As the girls disappeared around the bend, Melissa turned to me. Her eyebrows were raised so high that they were practically in her hair. "Were those girls just running with their bikes?"

"Looked like it," I said.

"Why wouldn't they just ride them?"

"The witch's curse strikes again," said Anthony. "Folks here are so used to doing everything magically that they don't know how nonmagical things work. It's kind of sad."

"I always thought bicycles were pretty self-explanatory," I said.

"Oh, that's nothing. You should see how people try to milk cows here." Anthony smiled mischievously. "It turns out all the tickling in the world won't make a cow give even one drop of milk."

I hoped the gnome was joking, but before I could ask him, he hurried off down the path. I had no choice but to follow him.

Chapter Five

When we came out on the other side of the forest, I got my first glimpse of the village. As much as I hated using the word, I had to admit the place was adorable. I could almost imagine the seven dwarves whistling as they went off to work.

"This is amazing," Trish whispered beside me. She pulled a notebook out of her bag and started furiously writing notes as she walked. No doubt her English paper was going to be epic.

I, on the other hand, hadn't even had a chance to start my paper yet. Now that Anthony and Dr. Bradley weren't using their magic to make sure I passed all my classes, I had to find time to keep up with schoolwork on my own. After years of not worrying about tests and papers and homework, getting back into school mode wasn't easy. Hopefully, I'd get the hang of it soon.

As we got closer to the village, I realized it only looked cute from a distance. The houses, which were clearly made out of gingerbread, were rotting and moldy, the gardens looked gray and lifeless, and the air smelled like a mix of manure and old fruit.

"Ewww!" Melissa sang, crinkling her nose.

"Is this all because of the magic fading?" I asked.

Anthony nodded. "Magic was woven into the villagers' lives. When it started to disappear, everything else started falling apart too. Which reminds me—once I drop you off at the palace, I'll need to be on my way. The longer I stay here, the weaker my own magic will get."

By now, I was used to Anthony disappearing during my adventures, but this time I wished he could stay. It felt right, somehow, for him to be with me if I found out anything about my parents. But I'd just have to fill him in later.

As we got closer to the village, I spotted the palace perched on a hill just beyond it, like a dull gray tiara. The palace was such a depressing sight that I went back to studying the village. I noticed a few brightly colored banners strung from some of the rooftops.

"Are they getting ready for a parade?" I couldn't imagine what a land in this kind of shape could be celebrating.

Melissa's face lit up. "Maybe they're throwing us a welcome party!"

Anthony and I exchanged knowing looks. I couldn't remember the last time someone had thrown a celebration to welcome me, but I let Melissa enjoy the idea.

Meanwhile, Trish was taking everything in with enormous eyes. Each time she blinked, I could practically hear the *click* of a camera as she memorized every detail.

As we continued along the road, we spotted a couple of teenage boys coming toward us with fishing rods slung over their shoulders. The boys looked almost like your typical fairy-tale peasants—with clothes made out of burlap and leather—except for their hats. One was wearing a cap made of dirty old socks, and the other had a leather hat that had been patched with leaves. I had a feeling the strange headgear was another sign that the villagers were having a hard time figuring out how to live without magic.

"Catch anything?" I called to the boys, thinking I might get more info about this weird land.

They stopped walking and gave us all suspicious looks. "You're not from around here," one of them said from under his sock hat. "Otherwise, you'd know that no one's caught anything in more than a year. We keep trying, but it's useless."

"Because of the dwindling magic?" I asked. I could see Melissa eyeing the boys, clearly trying to figure out if they were cute or not. Their faces were covered in so much dirt that the two of them might have looked like ducks underneath. Meanwhile, Trish was still scribbling away.

"What else would it be?" said the other boy before spitting on the ground. Apparently, these boys had the manners of ducks too. "No magic means no magic fish."

"What do you eat, then?" Trish jumped in, her pencil poised in midair.

"Well, we tried farming, but no one in the village could figure out how to do it. These days, we mostly have to depend on the festival," one of the boys said. Before I could ask what he meant, he took a step toward me and said: "So who are you?"

I opened my mouth to do my usual introductory spiel, but Anthony jumped in first.

"We're just passing through," he said a little too loudly. "In fact, we should be hurrying along." Then he herded me, Trish, and Melissa down the road.

"What was that all about?" I said as Anthony pushed us in the direction of the palace.

"Look, I didn't want to be the one to tell you this,"

said Anthony, "but adventurers aren't all that popular around here."

"What? Why?" I'd met creatures that were skeptical about adventurers, but I'd never been to a place where I had to hide my identity. I did enough of that in my regular life.

Anthony tried to keep walking, but I pulled him to a stop and made him face me. His chest was heaving as he tried to catch his breath after walking so fast on his short legs.

"Tell me what's going on," I said. "Why are you and Dr. Bradley acting so weird today?"

Anthony glanced over my shoulder at Trish and Melissa. Then he took my arm and gently pulled me aside. "It's because of your mom and dad," he said softly. "They're the reason people here don't trust the Committee."

I stared at him. All this time he'd claimed he didn't know anything about my parents' final mission, and now it turned out he'd been holding out on me.

"Your parents were the last adventurers sent here," Anthony went on. "They were asked to deal with Ilda, who was a problem even then. She loves to play tricks on people. The magic-sucking curse is just her biggest one. You won't believe what she did to the king and queen—"

"My parents," I reminded him. "*How* are they involved in all of this?"

"After your parents disappeared, the magic started to disappear too. Even though Ilda is clearly behind the curse, the timing was a little too coincidental. You wondered if the two things were connected. So did the villagers. That's why they didn't want the Committee's help anymore, and that's why they have a grudge against adventurers."

"Jenny?" I heard Melissa say, but I ignored her. I needed to get the whole truth.

"So you're saying that no one here wants my help, and they think my parents were in cahoots with an evil witch?" No wonder Dr. Bradley had wanted to prepare me for the mission.

"Basically," said Anthony.

"Um, guys?" said Trish, a note of panic in her voice. "Is that normal?"

Anthony glanced over my shoulder and his rosy face went pale. "An angry mob heading straight for us?" he said. "Nope. I would say that's not normal at all."

Chapter Six

"Get us out of here!" I cried as the villagers rushed toward us like a fuming snake.

Anthony gathered us all together and—*Pop!*—we were instantly on the palace steps. I could still hear the mob's cries below. In fact, the villagers sounded even angrier, probably because we'd used magic in front of them when they didn't have any of their own.

As Anthony ushered us inside the palace, I expected guards and servants to greet us, but there was just an old man with a few wiry hairs on his shiny head. His uniform was a sad, faded red, and most of its buttons had been replaced with random things like rocks and pieces of metal and what looked suspiciously like small bones.

"The princess has been expecting you," he said, his voice thin and scratchy. He led us down a dank hallway that smelled like rotting turnips. We had to weave around bowls of water that had been left out in front of almost every window.

"What's with all the bowls?" I finally asked.

The servant sighed. "I keep hoping the sunlight will bring the water to a boil, but so far it has not worked. I promised Her Highness that I will find a solution, and I shall keep trying until I do."

Anthony gave me a knowing look. This kingdom really was in pathetic shape without magic. People couldn't do even the most basic things for themselves. Finally, the servant ushered us into a cold chamber with only a rocking chair and a throw rug in the center. Princess Nartha was poised in front of a dusty window, standing so still that at first I thought she might be a statue. Then she let out a long sigh.

"Wait here," I told Trish and Melissa. Neither of them looked happy, but they stayed put.

After I'd left my friends safely in the corner, I followed Anthony to meet the princess. She had the stooped posture of someone old and weathered, and her clothes hung on her like oversized curtains, so I was surprised to see that she was actually only a few years older than me.

Something that sounded like cooing echoed above my

head. I glanced up and spotted a handful of pigeons roosting in the rafters. Luckily, they were on the other side of the room so I didn't have to worry about getting "rained on."

"Stop right where you are!" Princess Nartha cried when Anthony and I had taken a few steps.

My foot hovered above the rug. Maybe the princess had a thing about people wearing shoes in the palace. Not that it would matter in a place as dirty and run-down as this.

"Please," she said. "Come around this way." She waved us along the outer edge of the room until we met her in front of the window.

"Your Highness," I said with an obligatory bow. I nudged Anthony, and he reluctantly bobbed up and down. Hunger definitely did not bring out the gnome's polite side.

"So, you've arrived," Princess Nartha said with a sigh. Her greenish skin and under-eye circles made her look like she hadn't slept in weeks, but otherwise, her face was impossible to read. I couldn't tell if she was glad to see us or if she was going to cook us for dinner.

"Next time, you might want to send a greeting party instead of an armed mob," I couldn't help saying.

The princess shrugged under her too-long cape. "I didn't send the mob, but my people are wary of your kind." She looked me up and down. "The Committee told me your parents were the last adventurers sent here. I'm surprised you would show your face after what they did."

I clenched my fists so tightly that they shook. "You're wrong. There's no way my mom and dad had anything to do with your magic disappearing."

"I want to believe you." Princess Nartha walked over and rested her hand on the back of the rocking chair. "My mother and father put their faith in the Committee for years. But now my parents are gone, and my kingdom is dying."

"I was sorry to hear about the king and queen," said Anthony, sounding oddly sincere.

The princess nodded as she stroked the arm of the rocking chair. Then she knelt down to run her fingers over the edge of the rug.

"Thank you," she said. "I only hope they're not in pain like this. I do what I can for them, keep them clean and safe, but…" She shook her head.

"Wait," I said, studying the well-polished chair and the plush woven rug. "*Those* are your parents?" I'd seen people turned into frogs, frogs turned into goats, goats turned into dinosaurs, and a million other bizarre combinations, but I'd never heard of anyone being turned into a rug. Suddenly the phrase "letting people walk all over you" had a totally new meaning.

The princess stood up. "One of Ilda's jokes. She said my parents were as interesting as furniture, and then she cursed them." Her eyes locked on mine. "That was why your mother and father were called here, to help return my parents to their rightful forms. But they failed."

I swallowed. I couldn't blame the princess for being bitter. After all, I knew what being left alone in the world felt like. But there had to be a reason my parents had failed the mission.

"I'm sorry," I said. "I promise I'll fix things."

"You are my last hope," said the princess, shaking her head like she wished that weren't the case. "I've lost nearly all control of my land. Thanks to Ilda's festival, my people are more loyal to her than they are to me. Once the magic is gone completely, I'm afraid the village will turn on me."

"What is this festival everyone keeps talking about?" said Anthony.

Princess Nartha sighed. "The Humiliation Festival. It's a yearly event now, a chance for Ilda to torture my people. I tried to put a stop to it at first, but these days it's the only way for many to get food for themselves and their families."

The princess's shoulders now drooped so much that I was afraid she might sink right onto the floor. "Can you tell us more about the Three Impossible Tasks?" I asked.

The princess went back to her spot by the window. I could imagine her standing there for hours, looking down at her dwindling village. No wonder she was acting so depressed.

"I'm starting to believe they truly are impossible," she answered. "When the curse first began, all the able-bodied people in the land tried their hands at the tasks. Each year, children who are old enough attempt them. But only one person has ever gotten beyond the first task."

"Who?" said Anthony.

A voice rang out in the hall: "Me!" It was followed by loud clanging.

Princess Nartha rolled her eyes as the sound drew nearer. "Yes," she said. "Sir Knight is the only one who has ever completed two of the tasks. And he will never let you forget it."

Clang. Clang! CLANG!

I turned just as the shiniest person I'd ever seen came through the doorway. Blinding armor covered every inch of his body. Each step he took made me think of the time a family of lemurs got loose in the pots and pans cabinet in Aunt Evie's kitchen.

The knight stopped, bowed to the princess—*Clang!*—and flipped up his helmet—*Ding!* I had to admit he was as handsome as a knight could be. I could see Melissa's eyes sparkling from all the way across the room.

"Fair maidens," Sir Knight said, bowing to Trish and Melissa. *Clang!* Before coming forward—*Clang, clang!*—and dipping into another bow in front of me. *Clang!*

I was starting to get a serious headache.

A door on the far side of the chamber opened and the old servant scuttled in. "Your Highness," he said. "Princess Aletha wishes to greet our guests."

"Very well," said Princess Nartha. "Give us a moment to prepare." She turned to Sir Knight. "Remember what you promised me."

Sir Knight bowed—*Clang!*—and then straightened up. "I will be perfectly silent, Your Highness." Then he froze like he was made out of nothing but metal.

Before I could ask what was going on, the door opened again and Sleeping Beauty walked in.

Seriously.

Princess Aletha looked exactly like I imagined the Disney cartoon would if she were turned into a real, live person. Impossibly bouncy, golden hair. Milky skin and perfect features that didn't need a hint of makeup. And a flowing, pink dress that seemed to swirl even when she was standing still.

From the look on Melissa's face, I could tell she was instantly suspicious of this gorgeous newcomer.

"You must be the adventurer!" Princess Aletha said in a melodic voice. She rushed over and wrapped her arms around me in a lilac-scented hug. "Thank you so much for coming to help our kingdom."

Now this was the kind of welcome I could get used to.

"I hope I can help, Your Highness," I said, giving her a little bow.

"Please," she said, taking my hands in hers. "Call me Aletha." She glanced over at the other people in the room and her eyes stopped on Sir Knight. He was still standing perfectly still, but he was gazing at the princess like she was his favorite kind of ice cream.

Aletha let go of my hands and turned toward the knight. "Hello again," she said with a shy smile.

The knight blinked back at her. There was no doubt

that these two seriously had feelings for each other. I could practically see pink hearts floating in the air between them.

Suddenly, the spell was broken as Sir Knight's eyes widened and he let out a cry: "Maiden!"

Then he lunged forward, grabbed me in a metallic grip, and threw me to the ground.

Chapter Seven

I hit the floor like a can of soup, my head thumping against the cold stone. Sir Knight had me pinned down, his metal-covered hands crushing my shoulders. For some reason, he was humming heroic-sounding music as he shielded me with his body.

My instincts kicked in, and I surveyed the room for danger. Nothing.

I squirmed out from under Sir Knight's grasp. "Why'd you do that?" I asked. He was still humming a song that could have been the soundtrack for an action movie.

"There was something falling from the ceiling," he said. "I was trying to save you."

The sound of gnomish laughter echoed through the chamber. "It was a feather," Anthony said through his giggles. "Good thing he saved you from it, Jenny-girl. You might have sneezed to death!"

Sure enough, a pigeon feather was lying on the floor near my head. I brushed Sir Knight away as he tried to help me up. "Thanks, I got it."

Then I heard Melissa let out a little cry. "There's something wrong with the princess!"

I spotted Aletha sprawled on the floor, clearly unconscious. "What's wrong with her?" I asked, rushing over.

"Alas, it was my fault," said Sir Knight, clanging alongside me. "I startled her, the poor sleeping beauty."

"More like *fainting* beauty," Princess Nartha muttered as she knelt beside her sister. She glanced up at me. "Aletha has a mild but very dramatic illness. The slightest scare makes her swoon. That is why I've requested that Sir Knight remain absolutely still around her."

"I couldn't help myself, Your Highness!" he said. "A maiden was in danger."

"Yes," Princess Nartha said dryly. "Jenny, I suppose we are now both indebted to Sir Knight. Just yesterday he saved me from a swooping pigeon."

"All right, folks. Step aside. I can help her," said Anthony, reaching for the pouch of medicines he always wore around his waist.

Princess Nartha waved him away. "She'll be all right.

We simply need to wait until she awakens."

As if on cue, Aletha started to stir. Instantly, Sir Knight went into statue mode again.

"Oh," she said, glancing at all of us gathered around her. "I am so embarrassed. I didn't mean for everyone to make such a fuss."

"Aletha," I couldn't help saying, "I have a question. How do you feel about spindles?"

"Spindles?" she said, slowly sitting up. "I must admit, I avoid them because of my delicate disposition. If something so much as scratches me, I instantly faint away." Aletha's eyes locked on Sir Knight's again. "It's ever so tiring."

Well, that explained *that* particular fairy tale. Trish was smiling triumphantly as she hunched over her notebook. No doubt there'd be a very interesting bit about the Sleeping Beauty tale in her paper.

"Sorry to interrupt," Anthony said. "But since Princess Aletha is better now, can we get back to business?" I could tell he was itching to get out of here. Either to conserve his magic or—more likely—to go tear into the candy Trish had given him. "Princess Nartha, if I leave Jenny and her companions here, will they be safe from that mob?"

I glanced out the window. Sure enough, dozens of

villagers were still coming toward the castle, armed with pitchforks and shovels and rolling pins.

"I will speak to my people," said Princess Nartha. "I promise they will not harm your friends. But when it comes to Ilda, there is no protection I can offer."

"Don't worry about that," I said. "I'll handle her."

Princess Nartha shrugged her hunched shoulders. Clearly, she didn't think I had a chance. That made me even more determined. I'd dealt with all types of witches— sparkly, warty, good, and wicked—and I knew I could handle whichever kind Ilda turned out to be.

"I guess I'm done here," said Anthony. He glanced at me, and for the first time I could remember, he seemed reluctant to leave. "You're sure you'll be okay, Jenny-girl?"

Finally, I realized why he was so worried. My parents had come to the Land of Tales thinking they'd be fine, and they'd never returned. Of course, if Anthony was really so concerned for my safety, why had he agreed to bring Trish and Melissa along? But I guess when it came to the promise of candy after all that celery, the gnome just couldn't resist.

"I'll be fine," I told him. "If I need you, I'll call."

He nodded, gave my elbow an affectionate pat, and—*Pop!*—disappeared.

"Now," I said, turning to the princess. "Where is that witch?"

Chapter Eight

Before we left the palace, Aletha gave each of us a warm
hug. "You will succeed. I know you will," she said in my
ear. Having her vote of confidence made me feel more
optimistic. If there were answers here about my parents,
I would find them.

"Here," she added, reaching into the folds of her gown.
"My little friend will help you on your journey. He has been
a great source of comfort to me during these hard times."

She stuffed something small and squirming into my
hand. I almost shrieked when I realized it was a mouse.
His fur was the same bright pink as Aletha's gown, and he
had a sparkly collar around his tiny neck.

"Um, thank you," I said, forcing myself to smile as the
mouse tried to run up my arm.

"Leonard, stop that!" Aletha said, laughing.

The mouse, who clearly understood human speech,

stopped scampering around and sat obediently in my palm. Since I had no idea what to do with my new woodland creature, I tucked him into one of the pockets of my bag and figured I'd worry about him later.

After Aletha and Sir Knight exchanged longing glances, the princess rushed away to the safety of her chambers before the mob outside got close enough to startle her back into dreamland.

When the old servant opened the door leading out of the palace, we practically smacked right into a wall of angry villagers.

"There they are!" someone yelled as all eyes glared at me, Trish, and Melissa.

"Please," Princess Nartha said, holding up her thin hands. "They're here to help us." Her voice was so soft and unsure that no one appeared the slightest bit convinced.

"We don't need their help!" someone else called. "Last time strangers came to our land, they took our magic away."

"That's not true!" I said. "My parents had nothing to do with the curse."

I realized I'd made a huge mistake as all eyes zeroed in on me and the shouts got even louder: "Those traitors were your *parents*?"

"Why should we trust you when they betrayed us?"

I could practically taste the anger in the air. The crowd started pushing forward until we were pinned against the door of the palace. The villagers were so close that I could smell their sweat. It reminded me of the stench of merpeople.

"What do we do?" said Princess Nartha, her eyes wide with fear. So much for her guaranteeing our safety.

I turned to the old servant. "Quick, get Princess Nartha out of here."

He nodded and shuffled along, herding the princess back inside. She didn't put up a fight, probably because she didn't have much left in her.

"I know!" said Melissa. "A cheesy saying should do the trick." She grabbed a fortune from her pocket and announced: "'A closed mouth gathers no feet.'" Her forehead crinkled. "Wait, what does that mean?"

Someone in the crowd grabbed my arm and tried to yank me toward him. I realized he was one of the boys I'd seen fishing earlier. His face was cleaner now but looked just as ugly since it was twisted into a snarl.

"We won't let you destroy what's left of our land," he hissed.

As I tried to break free, ready to kick him in the shin, a loud *Clang!* rang out beside me.

"Unhand her, ruffian!" said Sir Knight.

Then the knight's sword swished through the air right in front of my face, barely missing my nose. The boy holding on to me jumped back, releasing his grip. I'm sure the boy's arm was mighty thankful its owner had good reflexes.

"Let the damsels pass!" Sir Knight said, waving his sword around. The gesture was supposed to be menacing, but since the knight managed to smack himself in the helmet with the hilt of his sword—*Dong!*—it didn't quite have the desired effect.

The mob burst out laughing, and I couldn't help exchanging amused looks with Trish and Melissa. Sir Knight might have been brave, but he wasn't all that skilled (at least not without the help of magic). And judging by the crowd's reaction, he wasn't all that popular. But now that the villagers in the mob were laughing, I had a chance to reason with them.

"Everyone!" I called. "Please listen to me for a second!"

The last of the laughter died down, and the crowd glared at me again.

"We don't want to listen to anything you have to say, Adventurer," an old woman spat while other people murmured among themselves.

"I don't blame you for hating me. If I were you, I'd hate me too." I tried to make eye contact with as many people as possible. I'd learned it was easier to get people to listen when you were staring them down. "But I swear I'm only here to help. I'm going to attempt the Three Impossible Tasks to see if I can restore your magic and save your land. If I fail, I'll leave and not bother you again. I promise!"

The crowd quieted down a little bit, but I could tell the villagers still didn't trust me.

"You only have a few days left before your magic is gone forever," I tried again.

"Thanks to your parents!" someone called out.

I swallowed and pretended I hadn't heard that. "No one else has been able to complete the tasks. Don't you want to at least give me a chance? What do you have to lose?"

It wasn't my most uplifting speech, but it seemed to actually get through to people.

"Nothing ventured, nothing gained!" I added. The cheesy saying, as usual, did the trick. People finally settled down and the murmurs died out. "Thank you. Now, please, let us pass. We need to find Ilda and set things right."

Sir Knight had managed to regain his composure and was now standing next to me. Even if he was a bit of a joke, he still had a sword. Slowly, people started to step aside.

As we made our way through to the other side of the crowd, I caught Trish and Melissa looking at me with wide eyes.

"What?" I said.

"You were amazing, Jenny!" said Melissa. "You totally took charge!"

"I can't believe we got to see you in action," said Trish. "It was so exciting."

I shrugged like it was no big deal, but I had to admit that hearing their compliments felt great. After years of not being able to share this part of my life with my friends, they could finally see what it was like to walk in my adventuring sneakers.

Chapter Nine

"Thank you again for showing us the way, Sir Knight," said Melissa, fluttering her eyelashes in his direction. We had managed to make it to the other side of the village without any more scrapes.

Clang. Clang. Clang. "The pleasure is all mine," the knight declared.

"You didn't have to go to all this trouble," I said. "We could have made it to the witch's house by ourselves."

"Nonsense!" The knight flipped up his helmet. *Ding!* "I couldn't allow three fair maidens to put themselves in harm's way."

Melissa elbowed me in the ribs. "Isn't he cute?" she whispered.

"He's clearly taken," I whispered back, thinking of the way he and Aletha had drooled over each other. "Not to mention too old for you."

Clang. Clang. Clang.

"Sir Knight, do you always wear your armor?" I couldn't help asking over the ringing in my ears.

The knight nodded, his usually proud shoulders drooping. "Alas, Ilda cast a spell on me that prevents me from ever taking off my armor."

"You can *never* take it off?" said Trish, scratching her head with her pencil. "Not even when you go to sleep?"

"Never," said Sir Knight. "I suppose I shall wear it until I die." He let out a soft laugh. "It's not all bad, I suppose. I *am* able to remove my helmet. And I'm prepared for battle at any moment."

"But what about Princess Aletha?" said Melissa. "If you didn't have your armor anymore, you wouldn't have to worry about scaring her all the time. Then you two could be together."

The knight let out a long sigh and started humming a mournful tune. I couldn't imagine how hard it must be on him, knowing that every move he made caused the woman he loved to pass out. Definitely not a recipe for a successful relationship.

"Don't worry," I told the knight. "I'm sure we'll be able to get Ilda to reverse her spell." And then my ears would finally get a break, I thought wistfully.

When we came to the end of the path, I spotted someone leaning against a giant rock. As we got closer, I realized it wasn't a some*one*. It was more of a some*thing*. An animal covered in thick fur, standing on its hind legs, and wearing—if my eyes weren't deceiving me—gym shorts.

"Is that a wolf?" Melissa whispered. "Dressed in workout clothes?"

Sir Knight drew his sword. "Fear not. I shall handle this." He started humming a heroic tune again as he rushed off down the path. *CLANG! Clang! Clang.*

"Come on!" I called to my friends, running after him. The last thing I wanted was to watch Sir Knight accidentally stab his eye out with his own weapon.

When I reached the end of the path, I spotted Sir Knight gesturing wildly with his sword. But when I get closer, I was surprised to see that instead of threatening the wolf, the knight was chatting with him as if the two were old friends.

"And then," Sir Knight was saying, "I told the crowd to clear the way to let the maidens pass or they would have me to reckon with. Instantly, the villagers fell to their knees and begged me to spare their lives."

"Good for you!" the wolf said. "Those villagers need to be reminded who's boss." The wolf glanced up as my friends and I came to a stop. He bared his teeth in a wide smile and licked his lips. "Who are these tasty morsels?"

"Now, Ralph," said Sir Knight. "I asked you to be courteous with these maidens."

"I *am* being courteous," said the wolf. "Or at least, I'd like to be *courting* them." He laughed at his own terrible joke.

I couldn't help rolling my eyes. Was this what fairy-tale wolves were like? How could Red Riding Hood stand talking to one for more than a second? Then I noticed that Melissa was giggling and self-consciously tucking her hair behind her ears. Maybe his methods did have an effect on some people.

"Sir Knight, we have to go," I said, ignoring the wolf's leering gaze.

"So soon?" said Ralph. He reached behind the boulder and brought out a dumbbell carved from wood. Then he started pumping iron in an obvious attempt to impress us.

"Wow, you're so strong!" said Melissa, tossing her hair over her shoulder. What was wrong with her? Was this meathead routine really working on her?

Meanwhile, Trish was sketching a portrait of the wolf in her notebook. "Mr. Wolf," she said, "do you know a girl who wears a red hood, by any chance?"

The wolf stopped his workout, his eyes suddenly shifty. "What are you implying? Has someone been spreading rumors about me?" Then he froze, his ears standing at attention. "I hear it," he whispered. "It's coming."

"What's coming?" I asked. Then I heard it, too. Something was running toward us at top speed. My first thought was more people "riding" their bikes, but this was different. This sounded huge.

The ground started to shake as the thing charged toward us. Meanwhile, Ralph's eyes had become perfect circles and drool was dripping from his chin.

"Dinner," he whispered.

"Ralph, no!" said Sir Knight. "Try to control yourself."

A second later, what had to be the most enormous rooster in the universe ran out from the bushes. It was at least the height of a basketball hoop.

The rooster took one look at us, let out a terrified crow, and charged down the path. I must have been seeing things, because I could have sworn the rooster was wearing a pink bonnet on its head and a leather saddle on its back.

Before I could even react, Ralph bolted after the rooster on all fours. He bounded about ten feet, looking like he was about to catch the rooster's tail in his teeth.

Suddenly the wolf's entire body snapped back like he'd hit an invisible wall. He flew through the air and landed on the ground with a dull thump.

"Ralph!" Sir Knight called, clanging over to him. "Are you all right?"

"One day," the wolf was muttering as he sat up, clearly dazed. "One day, I'll catch it."

"What *was* that?" I said. The last thing I'd expected to see in a fairy-tale land was a gigantic rooster.

"Ilda's steed," said Sir Knight.

"Steed?" Trish repeated. "Isn't that normally a horse?"

"Usually, yes," said Sir Knight. "But Ilda prefers that beast. She rides him all around the village. The saddle is enchanted, so the foul creature must do whatever Ilda commands."

Melissa giggled. "*Fowl* creature! Get it?"

Sir Knight looked at her blankly. Apparently, he wasn't a big fan of puns.

Meanwhile, Trish's face was glowing with excitement. "Of course! This all makes perfect sense."

I looked at her. "*What* about oversized, saddled poultry makes sense?"

Melissa was still giggling. "It sure did smell *fowl*! I heard it got kicked out of a rooster race for *fowl* play." Apparently, the wolf's terrible pun disease was contagious.

"It's something I came across in an Eastern European folk tale," Trish said. "A character flying around on a giant rooster. I thought it was a pretty weird thing to put into a story, but I guess it must have been inspired by that thing."

"That thing" had long since faded into the bushes, but Ralph was still staring after the huge rooster with crazed eyes.

"Once a day, Ilda has the creature run past here," Ralph said. "And every day, I get a little bit closer to catching it. If I keep training, someday I will."

"But what happened?" I said. "Why couldn't you keep running?"

"My chain. It's one of Ilda's curses," said Ralph, finally snapping out of his trance. "It only lets me go so far. That's why the witch sends that creature by here every day to torture me."

"I don't see a chain," said Melissa.

Ralph sighed. "It's invisible. But trust me, it's real." He clambered to his four feet, then straightened up so he was back to standing on two. Then he limped over to the boulder and started weight-lifting again. "Next time, I'll be ready," I heard him say.

I glanced at my friends and saw the same pitying look on their faces that was probably also on mine. I never thought I'd feel sorry for a slimy wolf, but whatever Ralph's personality faults, what Ilda had done to him was unbelievably cruel.

It was yet another thing we would have to set right.

Chapter Ten

After we'd left Ralph behind (once Melissa promised to go out on a date with him someday), Trish got right back into academic mode.

"Sir Knight," she said, notebook at the ready, "did you choose to become a knight or were you born into it?"

"*Choose* to become one?" he said, as if the idea were totally foreign to him. "I was born a knight. How could you suggest I could be anything else?"

Trish blinked. "Sorry if I offended you."

Sir Knight bowed his head. *Clang.* "My apologies," he said. "Being a knight is all I've ever known. It's not something I think about. It is simply who I am."

"And you're clearly good at it," I said, trying to smooth things over.

"Do you think so?" Sir Knight said, his face lighting up. "That means so much coming from someone as brave as you."

"Jenny," Melissa announced, "I've been working on a song for you. Do you want to hear it?" I had a feeling she was trying to show off in front of the knight, probably because he'd been paying more attention to me than to her. Sometimes Melissa could get weirdly competitive, but I knew she didn't mean anything by it. It probably wasn't easy having two super-talented parents.

"Sure." I plastered a smile on my face, hoping this song wasn't anything like the last one Melissa had subjected me to. That one had sounded like it had been written by a dying cat that had just learned to rhyme.

Melissa glanced excitedly in Sir Knight's direction before clearing her throat and singing in a high, sweet voice:

> *Jenny is an adventurer.*
> *She couldn't be any awesomer.*
> *She's helped by a gnome named Anthony.*
> *He likes to eat lots of beans jelly.*

The song went on and on, and I had to look at my feet to keep from cracking up. Melissa's voice was gorgeous, and the melody wasn't bad, but the words...weren't great.

When the song finally ended, Sir Knight clapped his

metallic hands as if the performance were the greatest thing he'd ever heard. *Clunk. Clunk. Clunk.*

"Splendid, maiden," he said. "Simply splendid!"

Melissa's cheeks flushed from the attention. Even Trish, who usually groaned the minute Melissa started singing, was applauding. I couldn't remember the last time my friends had looked so happy. Maybe bringing them along on the mission *had* been a good idea.

A few minutes later, we passed by a field where several kids were running around with logs tied to one of their legs.

"What are they doing?" I asked, watching the kids stumbling more than running. They looked determined to go as fast as possible, even if that meant wiping out every few steps.

"They're training for the festival," said Sir Knight. "The three-legged race is one of the most popular events."

"Why not just tie their legs to each other's?" said Trish, scratching her head with the end of her pencil again. I was afraid she'd scratch off some of her curly hair if she wasn't careful. "Wouldn't that make training easier?"

Sir Knight furrowed his brow. "Then it would be a four-legged race, wouldn't it? The logs are a good way to get used to having an extra leg."

"An extra leg?" said Melissa, her eyes widening in horror.

"Wait," I said. "Sir Knight, are you saying that the kids actually have three legs during the race?"

He nodded. "After Ilda works her magic, yes. The effect is temporary, of course, and only lasts for the day of the festival, but it's enough to make Ilda laugh. The more amused she is, the more generous she'll be with prizes. One year, I came in first in the dirt-eating contest, and I won enough food to feed myself and my brother for months."

Did Ilda really get her kicks from forcing people to eat dirt and watching kids stumble around on extra limbs? That qualified as a particularly horrible brand of evil.

"You have a brother?" Melissa piped up, looking hopeful.

"When is the festival?" I said loudly. We were *not* here to help Melissa's dating life.

"In three days," said the knight.

The last day of the curse. Figured. Big events often came at the same time during my adventures. Hopefully, I'd have completed the three tasks, brought back the magic, and gotten rid of Ilda long before the three days were up. Then no one else would have to be humiliated in exchange for food.

"Sir Knight," I said, "what can you tell me about the Impossible Tasks?"

His face fell. "Nothing, I'm afraid. Part of the curse is that you can't speak to anyone else about the specifics of the tasks." He hung his head and whistled a few sorrowful notes. "Alas, I barely even began the third task before I failed."

As we rounded a bend in the road, I spotted a cottage in the distance. "Is that Ilda's house?"

"It is, indeed!" said Sir Knight.

I'd expected Ilda's lair to be dark and ominous, so I was surprised to see a small, happy-looking cottage with a brick-red roof. Like the houses in the village, this one was made out of gingerbread, but unlike those, it looked fresh and—I had to admit—delicious.

Good thing Anthony was already gone, or we'd have a serious Hansel and Gretel situation on our hands.

As we got closer, something crowed loudly behind the house. A second later, the bonnet-wearing monstrous rooster came around the corner. He cocked his head to the side at the sight of us. Then his eyes widened in fear, and he let out a deafening squawk. The Monsterooster staggered backward and fled around the house again where I could hear him clucking to himself. Clearly, he found us terrifying. The feeling was mutual.

"Okay, you guys stay here," I told my friends. "I'll go see this Ilda person."

"But, Jenny," said Trish, "this is a real witch we're talking about!"

"Exactly. That's why I don't want you near her. Sir Knight, will you watch over my friends and make sure they stay out here where they're safe?"

"It would be an honor." *Clang.*

I pretended not to notice Melissa pouting. I'd rather have my friends mad at me than turned into coffee tables… or worse.

I sucked in a deep breath, marched up the path, and knocked on the candy-covered door.

Chapter Eleven

"Fee, fie, foe, fum!" I heard someone say from inside the cottage. Then there was a loud giggle before the door flew open.

I stared at the witch, not because she was a hideous hag, but because she wasn't. She looked totally normal. Her face was round and pleasant; her gray hair was in tight curls around her head; and she wore a light pink cardigan with kittens embroidered on the front. She reminded me of my math teacher, only with fewer warts.

"Are you Ilda?" I said, making sure Sir Knight had brought us to the right house.

"I certainly am," the witch said, adjusting the clasp of a silver necklace that was peeking out from under her sweater. "And you must be the new adventurer. Welcome, welcome! It's always lovely to meet someone new. You never know what you might learn!"

I didn't buy the cheerful act for a second. I was tempted to grab the witch's shoulders and shake her until she told me everything she knew about my parents, but I had to feel out the situation before I did anything drastic. Besides, I wasn't a people-shaker by nature.

"I've been told that the magic in this land is almost gone and that you're the one to blame," I said instead.

"Oh dear. Blame?" Ilda said, like she was genuinely hurt. "I would hate to think people blame me when I'm just trying to help this land."

"How is stealing the kingdom's magic and forcing people to do the Three Impossible Tasks helping anyone?" I said.

Ilda smiled, and I noticed her front teeth were crossed over each other, like they were lying. "I'm just trying to challenge people to learn. After all, puzzles stretch our minds." Wow, she even sounded a little like my math teacher.

"What about the king and queen? How do I turn them back into their real forms?"

"Oh, those two," she said, shaking her head like she was talking about misbehaving kids. "I'm afraid we've never quite seen eye to eye. But if you're serious about changing them back, I'm sure we can work something out." She took a step forward, and her thick, old-lady perfume threatened to suffocate me. "And if you'd like to know more about your parents, Jenny, I can help you with that too."

I blinked. "How do you know who I am?"

She shrugged, playing with her necklace again. "I hear things. I do have large ears, you know." She turned her head and mumbled something under her breath. Her ears started to grow before my eyes until they were the size of pumpkins. Then—*Bam*! They exploded right in my face.

I shrieked and ducked, convinced I was covered in pieces of ear, but there was nothing on me. I straightened up and saw that Ilda was totally back to normal—ears and all—and smiling like she'd just won top prize at the state fair.

"You should have seen your face!" she said, tittering. "It was priceless."

Anthony had said that Ilda was crazy with a capital Q, but that was starting to seem like a serious understatement.

"Okay, here's the deal," I said, smoothing my hair back into a ponytail. "I came to get this land's magic back, so tell me what I need to do to complete the tasks."

"We're jumping right to business, are we?" said Ilda. She sighed like she was disappointed not to be able to pull any more exploding ear tricks. "All right, I'll show you. Come along!"

We left the cottage and walked up the road together past Sir Knight, who was shielding Trish and Melissa with his body and humming tunelessly the way people do when they're nervous.

"Sir Knight," Ilda said with a smile so fake it looked painful. "How nice to see you. Your armor is looking so wonderfully shiny today."

The knight's face turned bright red. Clearly, Ilda's curses were all a game to her.

Then her smile faded. "Oh my, I hope you're not planning to try the tasks again," she added. "Don't forget that you only get one chance to attempt the Impossible Tasks. Once you fail, I'm afraid it's over. You don't want to break the rules, do you?"

Sir Knight quickly shook his head. *Cling. Cling.* "No, I-I'll do whatever you say. Just please d-don't make me sit under my desk again."

"What is he talking about?" I asked.

Ilda just laughed and turned to where Melissa and Trish were standing with their mouths open, staring at the witch as if she were a movie star. "Friends of yours, Jenny?" she said. "Will they be accompanying you on your quest?"

I swallowed. I wanted to tell her that I'd be attempting the tasks on my own, but I knew Melissa and Trish would throw a fit. "Yes," I said finally. "We'll be doing the tasks together."

The witch's eyes twinkled. "How lovely. Just remember, if you go as a team, none of you may try the tasks again. This will be your only chance."

"I understand," I told Ilda, my voice oddly squeaky.

For some reason, I couldn't shake the feeling that Ilda was a cat ready to pounce, and the rest of us were unsuspecting mice.

Wait. Mice!

I peeked into my bag to check on Leonard. I couldn't believe I'd totally forgotten about Princess Aletha's gift. Luckily, the pink creature was sleeping soundly, curled up with an old tissue.

"And one more thing," I said to Ilda as I zipped up my bag. "You need to undo all the curses you've put on people, including Sir Knight."

The witch laughed. "My, you certainly are demanding. Just like my old students."

"Students?" I said.

"Oh yes," said Ilda. "I was a schoolteacher once. There was a time when I taught every single child in this kingdom."

Now Sir Knight's comment about being punished made a little more sense. He'd probably had this crazy witch as a teacher.

"Alas," Ilda went on, wistfully looking into the distance like a character on a soap opera. "The school mysteriously burned down one day and there wasn't enough magic to rebuild it."

She put on a good act, but I was willing to bet Ilda had set that fire. After all, didn't *she* have enough magic to rebuild the school? But that wasn't why I was here.

"Will you undo the curses or not?" I asked.

Ilda let out a trilling laugh, though I had no idea what was so funny. She was really creeping me out. "Very well!" she said. "If you complete the tasks, we can negotiate. And rest assured, what I said about helping you with your parents was true."

I tried to read her face, but her pasted-on smile told me nothing. "What's in it for you?"

"The pleasure of seeing people learn, of course. No one will be able to complete my tasks. They're called 'impossible' for a reason. But it's such a joy to see the villagers attempting the tasks and realizing they can't succeed." She giggled again and put her arm across my shoulders. I felt like a boa constrictor was wrapped around me.

I wrestled out of her grip and sped up. "Let's just get this over with."

"Patience, my dear! Hasn't anyone ever taught you that?"

I clenched my teeth, trying to keep my cool. Ilda was like every bad teacher in the universe rolled into one.

A few steps later, she came to a stop. "Ah, here we are."

We were at a low candy-cane fence that ran along one edge of the witch's property. I expected to see something that looked like an obstacle course set up for the Impossible Tasks, but beyond the fence was just grass and rocks and weeds.

The witch pointed toward the far-off trees, her painted nails sparkling in the sunlight. "Beyond the forest is a cave," she intoned, sounding suddenly serious and terrifying. "Answer the troll's riddle and you will find an object within the cave. Bring it to me, and you will be rewarded." Then she turned in the other direction. "Beyond the village is a lake. In its depths, you will find an object. Bring it to me, and you will be rewarded."

Finally, she pointed back in the direction of the palace. "Beyond the hills is a mountain made of glass. At the top, you will find an object. Bring it to me, and you will be rewarded." She turned to me, the now-familiar smile stretching across her face. "And if you don't…"

She didn't need to finish the sentence. We both knew
would happen if I failed. The land's magic would be gone
for good, and I would never find out what had happened
to my parents.

Chapter Twelve

"What are trolls like?" Trish asked as we made our way through the woods in the direction of the cave. It was blissfully quiet now that Sir Knight wasn't with us. I'd been relieved when Ilda had sent him back to the village as we'd set off on our quest. I didn't think my ear drums could take much more of his company.

"Trolls are pretty ugly," I said. "And they're usually grumpy. But they love riddles."

"Riddles?" asked Melissa. "I always thought trolls were kind of dumb."

"Nope," I said. "Anthony has a troll friend who sits around guarding a bridge and doing crossword puzzles all day. He gets every single answer right."

"That's fascinating." As usual, Trish was scribbling away. "I can't believe how much amazing stuff you've learned, Jenny. Why would you have ever wanted to quit being an adventurer?" Trish shook her head like she thought I was crazy.

I was about to answer when an odd feeling made me freeze.

I'd read about people getting a prickly sensation at the back of their necks when they thought they were being watched, but I always thought that was just a cliché. Now I knew it was for real. It felt like someone was running an ice cube down my spine. I whipped my head around, trying to spot the mysterious watcher. But no one was there.

"Jenny, are you okay?" said Melissa, poking me in the shoulder.

I blinked. "Yup. I'm great." I pushed thoughts of axe-wielding forest monsters out of my head. It must have just been my imagination. Then I forced a smile onto my face. "Race you guys to the edge of the woods!" I announced.

The three of us took off through the trees. As usual, Melissa pulled into the lead right away, her long legs flying. After a second, she grabbed some dry leaves off the ground and playfully threw them at us as we trailed behind her.

"Hey!" cried Trish. She scooped up some grass and tossed it at Melissa, but it only managed to blow back in her face and get caught in her glasses. The three of us burst out laughing and slowed to a walk.

As we kept going along the path, I couldn't help thinking how great it was to have my friends with me. It barely even felt like we were on an adventure. We were just joking and laughing like we always did.

Finally, we came out of the forest into a rocky landscape that looked like it had a cave hidden behind every bush.

"How are we supposed to find this troll guy?" said Melissa.

"That should help," said Trish, pointing to a wooden sign nearby with "Troll Habitat Ahead" written on it. Below that sign was a second smaller one: "Riddle Enthusiasts Welcome." And below that was a third sign with the words "The Tastier, The Better" written in tiny letters. I didn't want to know what that last one meant.

We followed along the path until, sure enough, we came to the mouth of a huge cave tucked into the hillside. We heard something lumbering toward us inside the cave, and then two squinty eyes peered out from the shadows.

"Who's there?" said a low, raspy voice.

"I heard you have an impossible riddle for us," I called back.

The troll let out a delighted grunt and shuffled into the light. Trish and Melissa both sucked in a breath. Even

I had to admit the troll was a sight. I'd expected him to be lumpy and hunched, but I hadn't expected him to be Smurf blue or to be wearing round, wire-rimmed glasses. He looked a lot less threatening than your average troll, but I wasn't going to let my guard down just yet.

"Oh my gosh!" said Melissa. "He's adorable!"

The troll froze. "Pardon me. Did you just say I was *adorable*?" he asked in a surprisingly proper British accent.

"I always thought trolls were gross and smelly and stuff, but you're so cute!" she went on.

"Mr. Troll," Trish broke in, pulling her notebook out of her pocket. "Would you mind answering a few questions for me? I'd love to know a bit about how you see your role in the magical community."

The troll was starting to breathe heavily, like there was water boiling inside him. "How dare you? You come to my cave and speak to me in such a disrespectful manner? It's simply barbaric! I am a troll. You are expected to fear me!"

Uh-oh. This wasn't good.

Melissa's eyes lit up. She grabbed a fortune from her pocket and read: "'Your happiness is intertwined with your outlook on life.'"

"My happiness is *what*?" the troll roared.

"Guys!" I said, jumping in front of my friends. "How about you let me handle this?"

"But, Jenny," said Trish, "we were just trying to—"

"I know. It's okay. I'll take it from here," I said. My friends both looked unhappy, but they fell silent. Just in time too. The troll's blue cheeks were starting to look purple.

"I have never been spoken to in such a way!" he cried. "Imagine, after years of working to appear as fearsome as possible, someone comes along and calls you 'cute' and lectures you on happiness. I *know* how to be happy!"

"Of course you do!" I said. "We're sorry. We're, um, not from around here. It won't happen again." I didn't add that besides his size, the troll was about as scary-looking as a goldfish. And he certainly didn't *act* all that happy.

"I should hope not!" the troll said, slinging his trademark troll club over his shoulder. It was polished and oiled so it shone. Clearly, this guy took a lot of pride in his troll responsibilities. "So you are here to answer my impossible riddle. Shall we begin?"

"Yes, please," I said. I waved for my friends to join me. This time, they didn't look quite as eager to talk to the troll.

He took a deep breath, and his cheeks started to go back to their original blue color. "You will have three guesses. Each time you guess incorrectly, I will grow angry and violent. I'm afraid I can't help it. Trolls are perfectionists. Wrong answers make us quite irritable." He sighed as if this trait were a huge burden. "If all three answers are wrong, I will rip off your limbs and eat them with my afternoon tea. Is that clear?"

I heard Trish and Melissa let out little gasps beside me.

"I guess we'll just have to get the answers right, then," I said. Maybe I was wrong about the goldfish thing. The troll might not look frightening, but he seemed totally serious about gobbling us up.

The troll stuck out a monstrous blue hand. "Incidentally, my name is Irwin. I think we should be properly introduced before I suck the meat off your bones."

"Um, it's nice to meet you. I'm Jenny." I took the troll's hot-dog-sized pinky in my hand and shook it. Then I introduced my friends. Melissa looked squeamish when Irwin offered her a finger, but Trish's professional side took over and she gave him a nice, firm fingershake.

"Let's begin." Irwin cleared his throat and held his head high, like he was about to start singing opera.

You'll hear me when you're lifted up and down.
You'll see me when a tree you've wrapped your
car around.
I'm sure to growl if to me you add an "o."
And if you hear me repeated, you've won the
game show!

The troll fell silent and took a step back, an expectant look on his blue face. I couldn't help thinking that his rhyming skills weren't much better than Melissa's. But I tried not to focus on that as I started to replay the words in my head.

"Oh, that's easy!" Melissa said after a second. "The answer's a—"

"No, wait!" I cried. But it was too late.

"—staircase."

There was a long moment of silence. Then Irwin's eyes turned red, and he let out a high-pitched shriek. "*Incorrect*!" He swung his shiny club around his head and hurled it at Melissa.

"Duck!" I screamed.

Chapter Thirteen

Melissa managed to dive out of the way just in time. The troll's club fell to the ground with a dull thud, right in the spot where she'd been standing.

I ran over to where she was sprawled on the ground, looking dazed. "Are you okay?"

Melissa nodded and let me help her to her feet. "Guess my answer was wrong, huh?" she asked with a weak smile.

I tried to laugh but was too frazzled to do anything more than cough. "Yeah, I'd say so. Next time, let's check in with each other before shouting out answers, okay?"

She nodded. "Sorry." I could tell she meant it.

"No problem." I meant it too. Well, mostly. I couldn't blame my friends for not knowing how things worked. I'd just have to keep a closer eye on them; that was all.

"Pardon me," Irwin called. "Do you wish to continue guessing or can I simply eat you now?"

"We'll keep guessing!" I called back. Melissa, Trish, and I gathered together again. "Okay, guys, no shouting out answers," I reminded them.

"Shall I repeat the riddle?" said Irwin.

"Yes, please, Mr. Troll," said Trish.

Irwin sighed and began again in a lilting voice:

> *You'll hear me when you're lifted up and down.*
> *You'll see me when a tree you've wrapped your car around.*
> *I'm sure to growl if to me you add an "o."*
> *And if you hear me repeated, you've won the game show!*

As I tried to think, I heard Trish mumbling the riddle to herself. Her eyes were closed in intense concentration. Since Trish was the most book-smart of the three of us, she was bound to have the best chance of getting the right answer.

"Well?" said Irwin.

Melissa and I looked at Trish expectantly. She opened her eyes and shook her head. "I-I don't know, guys. I guess it could be…maybe it's a…"

"I'm growing impatient!" said Irwin.

"A rock!" Trish cried.

A rock? That couldn't be right. Could it?

"*Incorrect!*" Since Irwin no longer had his club, he grabbed a nearby boulder and chucked it in our direction. I threw myself forward and bowled my friends to the ground just as the boulder bounced past us like a basketball.

"I'm sorry!" said Trish as we scrambled to our feet. Her glasses were almost hanging off her nose, but she didn't seem to notice. "When I couldn't figure out the answer, I panicked."

"It's okay. We still have another chance." I hoped I sounded more optimistic than I felt. I wasn't exactly looking forward to becoming a troll snack.

"Do you give up?" Irwin asked.

"Not yet." I ushered my friends behind me this time, hoping that might keep them safe, and faced Irwin head-on.

"Once more, then," he said. "And I must say, I truly am sorry to have to eat you if you fail. I think we all could have been friends." He cleared his throat and repeated the riddle one more time.

> *You'll hear me when you're lifted up and down.*
> *You'll see me when a tree you've wrapped your*
> *car around.*

I'm sure to growl if to me you add an "o."
And if you hear me repeated, you've won the
game show!

This time Trish and Melissa kept their lips tightly sealed. My mind churned. There was no safety net. If I didn't get this right, we'd all be turned into finger sandwiches.

I'd never been great at riddles—even word searches tripped me up—but I tried to push that fact out of my head. After all, if Sir Knight could get the answer right, surely I could, too.

Wait. Sir Knight.

How had the knight—clearly not the sharpest sword in the armory—gotten the correct answer? Maybe that meant it was really obvious. Or…maybe he'd never figured out the answer at all.

Excitement bubbled up in my stomach. That was it. It had to be.

"Ding!" I cried.

Melissa and Trish looked at me like my brain had just fallen out of my head.

"Jenny, what are you doing?" said Trish. "Do you have the answer?"

"Ding," I repeated. "That's the answer."

My friends looked at Irwin, clearly terrified, as he let out a low laugh. Then he raised his giant hands and... started clapping.

"Nicely done, Jenny!" he said. "I was starting to doubt you."

I didn't admit that I'd been having doubts myself. My knees felt rubbery and weak.

"But, Jenny, how did you know the answer?" said Melissa.

I shrugged. "If Sir Knight could answer the riddle, I figured it either had to be really easy, or he must have gotten it right by accident. He's always *dinging* and *clanging* around."

"That's brilliant!" said Trish.

"Lucky guess." I turned to Irwin. "Now, if you'll excuse us, we have an object to find in your cave."

"You mean this?" He held out what looked like a clear spray bottle.

As I took it out of his hand, I realized it *was* a clear spray bottle filled with cloudy white liquid. This was what we'd almost gotten eaten for?

I unscrewed the top of the bottle and sniffed the liquid inside. The scent was tangy and familiar, but I couldn't quite place it. It definitely didn't smell like something I'd want to drink.

"Are you sure this is it?" I said.

Irwin nodded. "That's what the witch put in my home."

"But wait, why is it still here?" said Trish. "If Sir Knight completed the task, shouldn't he have taken it with him?"

"Ilda returns the object here if the person fails to complete the three tasks." Irwin's shoulders sagged, and suddenly he looked like a lost little kid instead of a flesh-eating troll. "So I guess you'll be leaving me, then?"

I nodded. "We have to go do the second task."

He let out a long sigh. "I understand. It's just...it gets a bit lonely here. Back when there was still magic, I could transport myself to different parts of the land to see my friends. But now the magic is almost gone, and they're all such a long way off."

"If you hate that the magic is disappearing, then why are you helping Ilda?" said Trish.

Irwin shook his head. "I'm a troll. Guarding is in my nature. When someone gives me an object, I have no choice."

He looked so genuinely sad that I couldn't help reaching out and giving his giant blue leg a squeeze. "Don't worry," I said. "I'll get rid of Ilda and bring the magic back.

I promise." It occurred to me how many times I'd made that same promise since I'd arrived in the Land of Tales. Apparently, I liked putting even more pressure on myself.

Irwin picked up his club and hugged it to his chest. "I wish I could believe that, but I'm afraid my land is doomed. Still, I hope you succeed."

"Where there's a will, there's a way," I said. I barely cringed anymore when cheesy sayings came out of my mouth, but I could practically hear Trish and Melissa rolling their eyes.

"Very true," Irwin replied like I'd said something unbelievably wise. At least he looked a little less deflated than he had before.

I tucked the spray bottle in my bag—careful not to squish Leonard, who was still sleeping soundly—and we waved good-bye to Irwin before heading back the way we'd come.

"That was great," said Melissa. "I could do it all over again!"

It took me a second to realize that she was being serious. "Are you crazy? We almost got turned into troll food!"

"I know," she said, her eyes sparkling. "It was so exciting. Way better than sitting in school all day." She started singing softly to herself, putting the troll's riddle to music.

"How do you deal with being back in our boring old world, Jenny?" said Trish. "This place is amazing. I thought it would be like living in a fairy tale, but it's even better than that."

Now Melissa was humming a different tune under her breath and composing a song about our adventure. I swore I heard her trying to rhyme the words "troll" and "boulder" with each other.

I couldn't believe it. Did my friends not realize we'd almost been goners? Maybe there was a reason normal people weren't allowed to go on these kinds of adventures.

As we climbed over a fallen tree, I stopped in my tracks. The feeling was back, that prickle along my spine that made me think we were being watched.

"Jenny, are you okay?" said Trish, turning to look at me.

For a second, I considered telling my friends the truth, but then I had a way-too-vivid image of Melissa running through the woods, excited to greet our potential stalker with a tune. Keeping my mouth shut was probably safer, at least for now.

"I'm fine. Let's go." I tried to make my voice light, but inside I felt anything but. There was no question now; we were definitely being followed.

Chapter Fourteen

The farther we were from Irwin's cave, the less freaked out I got. Whoever was following us clearly didn't want to hurt us, at least not right now. Otherwise, they would have already tried. Most likely, Ilda or one of her spies was keeping tabs on us. The only thing I was sure of was that it wasn't Sir Knight, since we would have heard his soundtrack echoing through the woods.

"Jenny," Trish said after we'd been walking for a while. "Is there any way we could stop and get something to eat? I'm starving."

"There aren't really any restaurants around here," I told her.

"Well, isn't there a peasant who could take us in and feed us? You know, like in real fairy tales?" Trish's face looked dreamy, as if she were imagining a kind old woman bent over a big pot of bubbling stew.

"Sorry," I said. "Even if we found someone, I don't think they'd want to help us, not after the welcome we got at the palace." I rifled around in my bag and took out one of the granola bars I always kept for emergencies. "Will this work? It's a little smushed, but it's edible." I didn't mention that Leonard had started to nibble through the wrapper.

Trish didn't look thrilled, but she unwrapped the granola bar and bit off a hunk without comment.

We'd taken a few more steps before Melissa stopped. "Jenny, there isn't a bathroom anywhere, is there?"

Didn't she know heroes didn't have time to go to the bathroom? I pointed to a nearby shrub. "Can you make do with that?"

Melissa sighed and went toward the bushes with a resigned look on her face. I wondered if this part of the adventure would find its way into Trish's English paper. I wasn't sure Mrs. Brown would appreciate an essay on the bathroom habits of magical creatures.

Finally, we set off again in the direction of the second challenge. All I knew was that Ilda had mentioned a lake. I wished I'd thought to pack a bathing suit. Diving for magical objects in jeans and a T-shirt didn't sound all that comfortable.

Soon we passed by a farm where a few boys were running around in a circle and squealing like pigs.

"What are they doing?" said Melissa, just as the boys noticed us and started to come toward the rotting wooden fence. They were all stick-thin, like they hadn't had a good meal in months.

The smallest boy in the group was clearly the bravest since he marched right over to us while the others hung back.

"You're the adventurer," he said, looking me up and down.

I nodded. "That's me. What are you guys doing?"

"My brothers and I are practicing for the pig race," he said. "I came in third out of all the boys at the festival last year. This year, I'm going to win, and Ilda will stock our barn with grain." The boy was far too young to be worrying about feeding his family, but he was clearly taking the whole thing very seriously.

"Let me guess. Ilda turns you into pigs before you race?" I said.

The boy nodded. "It tickles a little, but it's worth it. Even if I do snort-laugh for days after."

I couldn't believe the way the boy was talking, like he didn't see anything wrong with what Ilda was doing. How could people live like this? It was the furthest thing from a fairy tale I could imagine. There was no way I'd let Ilda get away with it anymore. When I glanced at Melissa and Trish, they were obviously thinking the same thing.

"What's your name?" I asked.

"Jack Beanstalk," the boy said, flashing a crooked grin.

"Your last name is Beanstalk?" I said.

The boy shrugged. "Not really, but that's what they call me. Ever since I threw those beans out the window."

"Wait!" said Melissa. "You're *that* Jack?"

"Where's your beanstalk?" said Trish, scanning the area. She was practically bouncing with excitement.

The boy's eyes widened. "You've heard of it? It's not much to look at now that the magic is almost gone, but it used to be amazing. It grew overnight, almost all the way up to the sky!" His face fell. "Now it's not growing at all. It doesn't even have any beans on it."

"Who knows," I said. "When the magic comes back, maybe the beanstalk will get so big that it really will go all the way up to the sky." My friends and I exchanged knowing looks as Jack's face lit up again.

"I hope so!" he said. "Just think how many beans would grow on it then. We wouldn't be hungry at all!"

"Especially if you like golden eggs," Melissa chimed in.

Jack's face scrunched in confusion. "What?"

I elbowed Melissa. There was no need to spoil Jack's future adventures for him. "Jack," I said. "Do you think you could do me a favor and share this food with your brothers?"

I reached in my bag and almost yelped as Leonard nipped my finger. Luckily, I managed to pull out my remaining granola bars with all my digits still intact.

Jack's big eyes got even wider. "You're giving us your food?"

I nodded and put the granola bars into his hands. "And don't worry," I said. "You won't have to be turned into a pig again. I'm going to fix things. I promise." There I went again, promising things. I was a promise-a-holic.

Jack grinned and turned to run back to his brothers on his skinny legs. As I watched the kids tear into the granola bars like they were the best things in the universe, I knew I had to keep my promise. No matter what.

Chapter Fifteen

When we got to the lake, the three of us let out a collective "ew." The water was so thick and green that it reminded me of split pea soup.

Near the edge of the lake, I noticed an older man sitting in a rowboat that was perched in the bushes. He was swinging an oar around like he was trying to push the boat through the air.

"Hey there!" I said, going over to him. This man didn't appear completely sane, but maybe he could give us a hint about our task. "What are you doing?"

"It won't move," he said, huffing as he kept swinging the oar through the air. "Every day I come out here, hoping it'll work again, but it won't."

"What won't?" I said as Melissa and Trish came up beside me.

"The boat. It used to bring me out onto the lake every

morning and float around to all the best fishing spots. Now it just sits here, useless."

"Did it used to run on magic?" Trish asked.

The man stopped swinging the oar and frowned at her. "Of course," he said. "How else would it work?"

The three of us exchanged looks. "By putting it in the water and rowing it yourself?" Melissa said slowly, as if she were explaining the idea to a toddler.

"But what would protect me from the monster?" The man looked at us like we were crazy.

"There's a monster in the lake?" Trish's cheeks flushed with obvious excitement.

The man shook his head, pursing his already-wrinkled lips. "It's best not to speak of the creature, or it will come."

"But what kind of monster is it?" I asked. "What does it do?"

The man stumbled out of the boat looking ready to run, as if he expected the monster to appear at any second. "It lures you in," he whispered. "And then it eats you." He turned and hurried away, leaving his boat behind.

"You don't really think the monster eats people, do you?" said Melissa after the old fisherman had disappeared down the path.

"Probably not," I said, not wanting to scare her.

Instead of looking relieved, Melissa looked disappointed. "I've never met a flesh-eating sea monster before."

"We still might," said Trish, clearly trying to cheer her up.

Obviously, my friends still didn't understand how dangerous missions could be. They were treating our adventure as if it were a game.

"Okay, we need a plan," I said. "We know there's an object somewhere in this lake." I turned to Trish. "What do people in fairy tales usually do in situations like this?"

Trish thought for a minute and then flipped through her book of tales. "A lot of times, they have to make a deal with a magical fish to help take them to the bottom of the lake."

"Well, we already know there are no magical fish here." I glanced at the murky water. Then I grabbed a pebble and tossed it into the lake. It sank and disappeared into the soupy grossness. I held my breath and waited, but nothing happened.

"Maybe that old man was wrong," said Trish.

Or maybe he was right, and a pebble wasn't enough to interest this particular monster.

I bent down and carefully dipped my fingers into the water, praying they wouldn't get bitten off. Instantly, something slimy flicked past me. I yanked my hand back, trying to see what it was. The water rippled and then quieted. Whatever lived in the lake, I'd definitely gotten its attention.

I bent down again, about to reach my hand in when—

Splash!

Something stuck its enormous head out of the water. It looked like a green worm with droopy eyes and nubby giraffe horns. Not quite the killer monster I'd been expecting.

"Nommy?" it said in a low, slow voice.

"Um, what?" I said.

As the monster swam closer, a glance at its fins told me just how huge it was, probably half the size of the lake.

"It's soooo cute," said Melissa. She seemed to think every creature in the Land of Tales was coo-worthy. Hopefully, no one would ever put her in charge of creating a petting zoo.

"Nommy," the creature said again as it studied us with its pale green eyes.

"Don't you think it looks like the Loch Ness monster?" Trish said behind me. "Maybe this is where the myth came from." I could hear her taking notes as she talked. Didn't her hand ever get tired?

"Aw, poor Nessie. He looks so sad," said Melissa. I didn't ask how she knew the monster was a boy.

"Excuse me!" I called to the monster. "Do you happen to know where we can find an object in this lake?"

"Nommy," he replied, slowly blinking his eyes. Oh well, it had been worth a shot.

"Do you think he's hungry?" said Melissa.

"Either that or he's looking for his mommy." I certainly hoped the creature wasn't wondering what we would taste like with a side of seaweed.

"He probably *is* hungry," said Trish, still focused on her notes. "I doubt there's much left for him to eat in the lake now that the fish are gone."

I looked around and spotted some berries growing nearby. A well-fed monster was much more likely to be cooperative. I had my friends help me gather some berries, hoping the monster didn't mind some fruit in his diet.

"Here comes the airplane!" I said, chucking a handful of berries into Nessie's mouth.

The monster flinched in surprise as the fruit hit his tongue. Then he opened his mouth wider, clearly wanting more. When our fingers were stained with juice and the berries were all gone, the monster finally looked happy.

"Now," I said. "Can you show us where we can find an object in this lake?"

"Hugsies," the monster said. His tail snaked toward us like a giant arm. "Hugsies."

"Look!" said Melissa. "What's that on Nessie's tail?"

I squinted and spotted something thin and metal wrapped up in the monster's curly appendage. "That has to be the object we're looking for. Nessie, can you give us what's in your tail?"

The monster's eyes narrowed, and he shook his head. "Hugsies!"

"He clearly wants something in exchange for the object," said Trish.

Melissa laughed. "I thought you were supposed to be the smart one. Obviously, he wants a hug!" She stepped forward and held her arms out like she was waiting for someone to put a straightjacket on her. "Here you go, Nessie. Come get your hug!"

"Wait!" I cried, but it was too late. Again.

The monster's tail lashed out and wound itself around Melissa's waist. Then his tail retracted and the beast dove under the water. Taking Melissa with him.

Chapter Sixteen

"Melissa!" I rushed into the water, feeling like my body was in slow motion. When I was up to my knees, I glanced over my shoulder to see Trish frozen in place. "Help me!" I cried. But she didn't move.

I kept pushing through the water until I was almost up to my waist. Then I sucked in a breath and got ready to dive where I'd seen Nessie disappear.

But at that moment, I felt the lake start to churn around me, and the monster broke the surface of the water only a few feet away.

"Melissa!" I cried as I spotted her still curled up in the monster's tail. She was coughing, which at least meant she was still alive.

"I'm fine!" she said, wiping green slime off her face. "I think he just got a little too excited."

"Hugsies," said Nessie.

"Ooh!" Melissa said. "You sure have a strong grip, don't you, boy?"

"Let go of her!" Trish yelled behind me, finally finding her voice.

"It's fine, guys," said Melissa. "He's not going to hurt me." Then her eyes widened. "Oh. He's...ouch."

"What's happening?" I said.

Melissa's face paled. "He's...squeezing...me..."

"Hugsies," the monster said. He coiled around Melissa protectively and swam farther out in the lake, reminding me of a little kid who couldn't wait to play with his shiny new toy.

"What are we going to do?" said Trish as she rushed into the water beside me. "He's going to squeeze her to death!"

I stared as Nessie twirled in a circle in the middle of the lake, Melissa nestled in his tail. She was struggling to get out of his grip, but she wouldn't be able to fight for long.

"Wait on the shore," I told Trish. I had no choice but to swim after the monster and hope he didn't start hugging me to death too.

I kicked off through the water, going as fast as I could. But as I got farther into the lake, I felt something nip at my legs. Once. Twice. Ten times.

"Ow!" I cried, slimy water pouring into my mouth.

Obviously there *were* fish in the lake, and they were anything but friendly. When one chomped into my ankle, I knew I had to turn back to the shore. I wouldn't do Melissa any good if I was chewed to pieces.

"What happened?" Trish cried as I stumbled out of the water, blood trickling down my leg.

"It's no use," I said, panting. "I can't swim out there. We have to find another way."

"But how?" said Trish, her voice shaking. "We don't even know how to deal with the monster."

My mind was spinning. "We have to think! How did Sir Knight do it?"

Trish pulled her book of fairy tales out of her bag again and started frantically leafing through it. "I don't know," she muttered to herself. "I just don't know."

I tried to imagine what Sir Knight must have done when he'd come to the lake. No doubt, he'd told Nessie just how brave he was. Then, after the monster had started turbo-hugging him, Sir Knight had probably waved his sword around without actually hitting anything except maybe himself.

"Clang!" I yelled. Nothing happened. "Ding!" The monster didn't even flinch.

What else could Sir Knight have done? Then I realized…

"He sang!" I said.

"What?" said Trish.

"Sir Knight probably did it by accident. He started humming like he does when he's trying to be heroic, and it had some kind of effect on the monster."

Trish snapped her book shut in excitement. "You might be right. But what do we sing?"

"I don't know," I admitted, limping back toward the edge of the lake. "Maybe any song is fine." I cleared my throat, self-conscious about letting loose my horrible singing voice, but there was no time to be shy. I opened my mouth and started singing the first song that popped into my head.

> *Jenny is an adventurer*
> *She couldn't be any awesomer.*

I couldn't believe I was belting a song about how awesome I was. Talk about embarrassing.

The minute I started to sing, Nessie's head snapped up, and he eyed me curiously.

"It's working," said Trish as the monster started drifting

toward us, a dreamy look sweeping over his face. "Keep singing, Jenny. Louder!"

I had no choice but to keep broadcasting Melissa's song in my off-key voice. For another moment, Nessie enjoyed the music. He was closer to the shore and his tail uncoiled a little. But when I hit a couple of wrong notes, he cringed and let out a howl.

"It's not working," I said. "My singing is just too terrible. Trish, maybe you should try?"

Trish nodded and started singing the same song. Her voice was a lot better than mine, but it was so breathy and quiet that it barely carried two feet. Nessie stopped swimming toward us and turned back to his prize.

"No!" cried Trish, clearly hysterical. "He's going to eat her!"

Suddenly a sweet, haunting voice rang out on the lake: Melissa's.

Instantly, Nessie's face relaxed, and he even started to hum along—as much as a giant worm with tiny ears *could* hum, anyway. Compared to him, I'd sounded like a Broadway star.

The monster floated toward the edge of the lake, and I could hear him purring like a motorcycle. He lifted his tail and carefully deposited Melissa on the ground. Then he murmured happily to himself, a little smile on his green face, and drifted away on his back.

I caught Melissa as she stumbled out of the water. She looked pale and terrified, but her voice was as gorgeous as ever.

When Nessie had disappeared under the water, Melissa's singing finally quieted. She gave us a little smile, took a step forward, and crumpled on the ground.

Chapter Seventeen

"Anthony!" I cried. "We need you!"

Trish looked ready to faint. "Melissa has to be okay! She just has to!"

"She'll be fine," I said, hoping that was true. At least she was still breathing.

A minute later—*Pop!*—Anthony appeared in front of us. When he spotted Melissa spread out on the ground, he dropped the carrot he was holding. Then he got to work, pulling all sorts of foul-smelling medicines from the pouch around his waist. A couple minutes later, the color was already starting to creep back into Melissa's cheeks.

"She'll be just fine," Anthony announced. Then he saw my bleeding ankle. "Looks like I missed some serious fun."

I let out a hysterical hyena laugh. "I guess you could say that."

As Anthony started bandaging my leg, I couldn't help looking out at the lake wistfully. The monster was gone, and with it the magical object. I'd take Melissa over an object any day, but that meant I'd have to find some other way to complete the task.

A second later, Melissa opened her eyes and smiled up at us. "That was awesome," she whispered.

I didn't know whether to smack her or to hug her. "Are you okay?" I asked.

"Are you kidding?" she said, slowly propping herself up on her elbow. "I'm great. That was the most exciting thing that's ever happened to me."

"You idiot!" said Trish, lovingly swatting Melissa's arm. "You almost died."

"No way," said Melissa. "And even if I had, at least it would've been worth it."

"What are you talking about?" I said. Maybe the lack of air had scrambled her brain.

"Ta-da!" said Melissa. She pulled something long and metal out of the pocket of her sopping-wet jeans.

My mouth fell open. "Is that—?"

"The second object!" she said, smiling triumphantly. "I snatched it out of Nessie's tail when he first grabbed me."

This time I didn't hesitate before throwing my arms around Melissa and hugging her tightly. After I finally let her go, I carefully examined the object. "But what is it?"

The metal was woven into a flat, round shape on one end, and then it extended down and formed a handle on the other end. It almost looked like a fly swatter.

Even Trish, who was usually full of ideas, had no clue what it could be. The shape of the object looked familiar, but I couldn't figure out where I'd seen something like it before.

"I guess Ilda will have to tell us when we bring it to her," said Melissa.

"Are you kidding?" I said. "No way. You guys aren't staying with me. I'm having Anthony take you home."

Melissa stared at me. "What are you talking about? I'm fine. We can keep going."

"She's right, Jenny," said Trish. She glanced at the bandage on my leg, and I could tell she was still a little shaken up. "Okay, maybe we won't go on the final task with you. But at least let us go back to the village and talk to some more people. This could be our only chance!"

"You mean talk to the villagers who chased after us with pitchforks? That's probably not the best idea." I had to face facts. It had been fun while it lasted, but bringing my friends on my adventure had been a mistake. "Sorry, guys. I wish you could stay, but this mission is just too dangerous. It's time for you to go home."

"That's not fair," said Trish. "There's still so much we haven't seen."

"And we were having a good time, weren't we?" Melissa added, her eyes suddenly wet with tears. "Please don't punish us just because I got myself hurt."

"I'm not punishing you. I'm protecting you! I could never forgive myself if anything bad happened to you guys. There's a reason adventurers don't bring regular people along on missions."

Melissa's face suddenly turned bright pink. "You think you're so special because you're an adventurer, don't you? You think we're not good enough to be here with you."

"What are you talking about?"

"Last I checked, we were actually helping you," Trish chimed in. "If not for Melissa, there's no way you would have gotten that metal thing out of the lake. But you just want to keep this place all to yourself."

I couldn't believe what I was hearing. "Don't you get it? I love you guys! I'm trying to keep you from getting yourselves killed." I couldn't handle seeing another monster practically strangle one of my friends. Once was more than enough.

Melissa wiped away a tear. "If you really cared about us, you'd let us stay. You wouldn't take this opportunity away from us."

I shook my head and turned to Anthony. "Can you take them home, please?"

He raised his orange eyebrows. "Are you sure?"

"Yes. And even if they offer you a wedding cake, don't bring them back here."

"You're the boss." He took Melissa's arm and grabbed Trish's before she could pull away. "Sorry, kiddos!" he said. Then there was a loud *Pop*! and they were gone.

I stood staring at the green lake for a long while, trying to tell myself I'd done what I had to do to keep my friends safe. And that they would forgive me. Eventually.

Chapter Eighteen

As I marched along to Ilda's house, I kept replaying the fight I'd had with Melissa and Trish. I couldn't help thinking how much more fun I'd had on the mission with them than on the missions I'd been sent on with Jasmine. But at least Jasmine understood what being an adventurer meant. She understood that our job was to help others, not to put them in danger.

My mother's bracelet shifted on my wrist. When I glanced down at it, I could almost hear it talking to me again. *If you find your parents, you'll finally have people in your life who understand you.*

The bracelet was right. Finding my parents and helping the Land of Tales were all that mattered. Everything else—the dance, my English paper, patching things up with my friends—would have to wait.

Still, I couldn't face the third task. Not yet. Not after everything that had happened at the lake.

First, I was going to get some answers.

As I charged toward Ilda's house, I realized I was going to pass the spot where we'd run into Ralph the slimy wolf earlier. I tried to hurry past without being noticed, but I should have known better than to think I could avoid being detected by a wolf's long ears.

"Why, hello there!" Ralph called out. "What happened to those delicious friends of yours?"

I didn't want to say anything, and luckily I didn't have to. Ralph dropped down on the ground and started doing push-ups in an obvious attempt to impress me.

"A young lass like you shouldn't be walking around in the woods by yourself," he said in between reps.

"Is that what you said to Red Riding Hood?" I couldn't help asking.

Ralph almost fell on his face. "Who told you that? Did someone say I knew her? Was it that mother of hers? You didn't believe her, did you? Did you?"

I hurried away, giggling to myself, my mood a little lighter. Apparently, smarmy fairy-tale wolves *were* good for something.

A few minutes later, I spotted Ilda's gingerbread house at the edge of the village. The Monsterooster was strutting around the yard, pecking at everything in sight. This time he was wearing a blue bonnet, which he was trying to shake off his head.

I hurried to the door before the rooster saw me and got scared all over again. I felt bad for the giant bird. Being Ilda's pet had obviously made him terrified of everything. But I didn't have time to think about saving poultry when an entire kingdom was at stake.

Ilda threw open the door before I could even knock. Her pink kitten sweater had been replaced by a blue cardigan with bedazzled cowboy boots all over it. Seriously, she and my math teacher had to shop at the same store. It was also clear that Ilda chose the rooster's bonnets to match her own outfits. Talk about animal cruelty.

"You're back!" Ilda said. "Have you given up so soon?"

"No way. In fact, I already have two of the objects." I patted my bag.

"Really?" Ilda smiled and played with the clasp of her necklace. "Then why are you here?"

"Because I'm not taking another step until you tell me what you know about my parents."

Ilda laughed. "Oh, my dear, what did I tell you about patience? I can't spill everything just because you asked me to. First, you need to complete all the tasks. Those are the rules."

"They're *your* rules," I said. "That means you can change them."

She opened her mouth and closed it again. "It's not that simple."

"Why not?" I demanded.

For a second, Ilda actually looked at a loss for words.

"Come on," I pressed. "I've been waiting seven years to find out what happened to my parents. Don't worry. I'll complete your stupid third task. But first I need to know what you know. What happened to them? Where did they go? Tell me!" I realized I was practically screaming. Even Ilda looked a little stunned.

"I do admire your determination." She sighed. "Very well. I suppose it can't hurt to tell you what I know."

She led me into her house, which was surprisingly cozy and smelled like hot cocoa. She pointed to a couple of rocking chairs by the fireplace, where a crackling fire was going. After seeing how run-down the rest of the land was, being somewhere so warm and inviting felt wrong. Then again, everything about the witch felt wrong.

"Now," she said, once we were both sitting, "where should I start?"

"Tell me what happened when my parents came here. And tell me the truth. No more games."

"Of course not!" Ilda said, like the idea had offended her. She leaned back and peered into the fire. "I remember when I first met them. It was right after the king and queen's transformation."

I bit my lip. Right. As if people spontaneously turned into furniture every day.

"Your parents came and demanded that I undo the spell," she went on. "But of course, I couldn't simply do that. One of life's greatest lessons is realizing you can't have something for nothing. So I told your parents to make me an offer and we could work out a deal."

"What was the offer?"

"There wasn't one," said Ilda. "Your parents refused. They said they didn't negotiate with bullies like me. Can you imagine? Calling me a bully when I'd spent years stopping children from being cruel beasts?"

Somehow I doubted the *kids* were the ones being cruel. "Then what happened?"

Ilda smoothed down her corduroy pants. "I tried to

reason with your parents, but they wouldn't listen. And then, *Poof*! They disappeared."

I leaned forward. "What do you mean?"

"Just what I said. One moment they were standing right here in my cottage. The next"—she snapped her fingers and sparks magically flew into the air—"they vanished."

"But why?"

Ilda shrugged. "I'm afraid I have no idea. But I know one thing for certain: I didn't cause it. They simply disappeared. I'll admit I was relieved. After that, I could continue with my plan without interruptions. I always plan much better when I have peace and quiet."

The Monsterooster let out a pitiful wail in the yard.

I clenched my fists into balls. I hated how lightly Ilda was talking about my parents vanishing. "So, why did you take the land's magic? What do you need it for?"

"That's like asking why we pursue knowledge!" said Ilda. She pointed her finger, and the flames in the fireplace roared. She was clearly showing off how much magic she had. "Isn't it enough to want something simply for the joy of having it?"

She acted like stealing magic was the same as Dr. Bradley getting pleasure out of filling his house with junk. But Dr.

Bradley would never hurt someone to add to his broken toaster collection.

"So, that's all you can tell me?" I said. "One minute my parents were here, the next minute they were gone, and you have no idea why they disappeared or where they went?" I couldn't tell if she was lying or if that really was all she knew.

"What did you expect, dear? That I'd draw you a treasure map? 'X' marks the parents? Where would be the challenge in that?" She leaned back in her chair and crossed her arms in front of her chest. "But let's be honest, Jenny. Have you ever considered that it might be too late to get your parents back?"

I blinked at her. "What are you saying? Do you know where they are? Do you know if they're okay?"

Ilda slowly shook her head. "I wouldn't know, of course. I already told you that I have no idea what happened to them."

I didn't believe her. She clearly knew something. And, worse, she obviously thought my quest was hopeless. But it couldn't be. My parents had to be all right. They had to.

"After all these years, no one has been able to track them down," Ilda added. "How can you expect to? You're just a girl. Sometimes, Jenny, we need to learn our own limitations."

I couldn't stand this conversation anymore. Obviously, I wasn't going to get anything out of Ilda other than mind games disguised as life lessons. I jumped to my feet and headed for the door.

"Where are you going?" she called after me. "I have one more thing to tell you about your parents."

Okay, that got my attention. I slowly turned around. "What?"

Ilda stood up, smiling as always, her crossed teeth smudged with orange lipstick. "They told me about you, you know. They said this was their last mission, and they couldn't wait to get back to their spunky little girl."

"What do you mean it was their last mission?"

"They were retiring, leaving adventuring for good, so they could be with you. Sad how things work out sometimes, isn't it?"

I stared at Ilda. It couldn't be true. Because if my parents had been planning to retire, my whole life could have been different.

With that thought burning my brain, I spun around and ran out the door. I had to get away.

Chapter Nineteen

As I left the village behind, the witch's words kept echoing in my head. Before I knew it, tears were dripping down my face.

I brushed them away. No. I wouldn't let her get to me. So what if my parents had been about to come back to me forever? That didn't change anything. Not really.

My mother's bracelet felt hot around my wrist, like it was trying to remind me of just how much I'd lost.

"Shut up, bracelet," I muttered.

I shook my head and kept going. I just had to focus on completing my mission. That was all I could think about. The sun was starting to sink toward the trees, which meant I had to hurry. As desperate as I was to complete the tasks, I wasn't about to go charging up a mountain in the dark.

Finally, I spotted a glass peak in the distance. It sparkled in the late-afternoon sun like a huge diamond. The closer

I got, the more impossibly tall the mountain appeared. Its transparent sides went almost straight up toward the clouds. How on earth was I supposed to climb it?

At the base of the mountain, I reached out to touch the glass, expecting it to be freezing. It was surprisingly warm to the touch. Now that I was up close, I could see that the mountain's face wasn't completely smooth. There were a few crags here and there, spots that I might be able to use as handholds.

I spit on my hands, rubbed them together, and got to work. After a couple tries, I managed to jump up and catch hold of a tiny ledge with my right hand. Then one with my left. I kept climbing until I was about twenty feet above the ground. Suddenly, I couldn't find anywhere else to grab on to.

As I hung from my fingertips, scrambling to find a handhold above me, my brain refused to focus on what I was doing. Instead, I found myself thinking about my parents again.

If my mom and dad were here, they would know how to climb this mountain. They'd been the best adventurers in history, after all. Past tense. Because no one knew where they were. No one even knew if they were still alive. What if Ilda was right? What if my search for my parents was hopeless?

My legs started to slide under me, and my hand was getting so cramped that I didn't think I could hold on much longer.

I clenched my teeth until they felt like they were about to break. Somehow, I managed to lift myself up just a little higher until—success! This time, I found not only a crevice but an actual ledge wide enough to stand on. I crawled onto it and pressed up against the glass, trying not to look down.

But my excitement was short-lived as I realized that above me, the rest of the mountain was now completely smooth. Not a single crack or crevice in sight. Unless I sprouted suction cups on my hands, I was stuck. Now what?

Then I heard screeching.

At first it was faint, but soon it grew louder and louder. *Skree. Skree. Skree!*

I glanced over my shoulder and almost screamed.

An enormous black bird was charging at me, its giant wings blocking out the sun. Its razor-sharp beak was easily the length of my entire arm.

As the bird got closer and closer, my brain was frozen. I couldn't climb. I couldn't jump. I just stood on the ledge, not knowing what to do. For some reason, all I could think about was how disappointed my parents would be if I got myself killed by a prehistoric bird.

Skree!

The bird was only inches away. Its beak was aimed right at me. I had to do something! Finally, I convinced my legs to jump.

I tumbled off the ledge and dropped through the air like a lump of clay.

When I hit the ground, it took me a second to realize I wasn't still falling. My body felt numb, almost weightless, and my eyes were swimming with black dots.

"Anthony," I mouthed, but no sound came out.

I tried to blink the spots away, but they just got bigger and bigger, until finally my vision blurred completely and all I could see was blackness. Then I was dreaming of witches and trolls and giant birds playing mini-golf.

Chapter Twenty

When I opened my eyes, it took me a minute to remember why I was sprawled on the ground with a shining glass mountain towering over me, and why my body felt like someone had used it for batting practice. Then I tried to remember why Jasmine was kneeling next to me with a careful smile on her face and a buffalo-shaped yarn necklace around her neck. She hadn't been there before, had she?

I struggled to sit up, but my head was throbbing and my body tingled like all my limbs had fallen asleep and were slowly waking up.

"Don't try to move," said Jasmine. "Once Anthony gets here, he'll fix you up and take you home."

"Home?" I whispered. "No. I have to finish the tasks."

A pained expression spread across Jasmine's face, and suddenly I realized the truth. There was no finishing the tasks. I'd attempted the third one, and I hadn't even gotten halfway up the mountain.

"I failed." The words came out weak and strangled. I'd let the Land of Tales down. I'd let little Jack and his brothers and everyone else down. All the promises I'd made had been for nothing.

Jasmine reached out and squeezed my hand. "It's all right, Jenny. I saw how hard you tried."

"What do you mean? You just got here."

She shook her head. "I've been here all along," she said. "I've been following you."

"That was you?" All this time I'd thought Ilda had been stalking me, and Jasmine turned out to have been the one watching me from afar. "But why?"

"To deliver your elephant earrings?" she said with a weak smile that told me she was attempting a joke. Then her face grew serious. "The Committee members asked me to. That's why they sent for me when I was at your house. They wanted me to keep an eye on you."

"You mean they wanted you to spy on me."

Jasmine started to object. Then she seemed to think better of it. "Well, I suppose that's one way of looking at it. They were concerned, that's all. This place is dangerous.

They wanted to make certain you were safe." Her smile faltered. "I'm afraid they won't be too happy to hear about your fall. I should have acted sooner, done something to help you."

"It wasn't your fault. Besides, I'm fine. And I'll be a whole lot better once I find a way to get rid of Ilda." Slowly, I managed to get to my feet, trying not to wince as my muscles screamed.

Jasmine jumped up to help steady me. "That's not your job anymore, Jenny."

"Of course it is. I can't let that witch keep messing up this land."

"You made a promise, remember?" said Jasmine, finally letting go of my arm. "You told the people here that if you failed the tasks, you'd leave right away."

I swallowed. Yes, I'd made that promise, but I'd also made one to Jack and to so many others.

"Princess Nartha contacted the Committee after you were at the palace and insisted that you leave her kingdom immediately if you failed," Jasmine added.

"But why?"

"Because that's what her people wanted and that's what she promised them. There's nothing else you can do."

My insides felt like they were deflating. Maybe it really was over. I'd tried the tasks and I'd failed. I'd tried to find my parents and I'd failed. What more could I do?

An urgent *Pop!* rang out and Anthony appeared. For once he wasn't holding any type of food, not even a diet snack. He just rushed over and pulled me into a hug.

"Are you okay?" he said.

"I'm fine." I tried not to yelp as he squeezed me tight. It didn't feel like I'd broken anything, but I probably resembled a bruised pear.

After Anthony let me go, there were actually tears shining in his eyes. "When I heard you were hurt…all I could think about was that day when your parents…" He wiped his eyes.

Just then, the most unwelcome sound I could imagine echoed above our heads: *Skree! Skree!*

The bird with a capital B was back.

"We need to get out of sight," I said, glancing around for somewhere to hide.

"Let's get you home," said Jasmine.

"No! I can't—"

Before I could even finish the sentence, Anthony grabbed my hand. With a *Pop!*, the Land of Tales faded around us. After a moment of psychedelic spinning, we were back in my bedroom.

Normally, I got a rush of comfort whenever I came home, but this time I felt empty. I stumbled across the room, pulled off my adventuring bag, and sank onto my bed.

"You need to rest up," said Anthony. "After the fall you had, some sleep will do you good."

"I don't want to sleep." The truth was, I didn't want to do anything. I'd never felt like such a failure. I'd let an entire kingdom down. I'd let my parents down. I'd even let my friends down. Maybe the Committee had been right to doubt me.

"Here," said Anthony, taking a pill out of his pouch of medicines. "Swallow this."

"I'm fine." I tried to push his hand away, but I was suddenly so exhausted that I could barely lift my arm.

"You're not fine," said Anthony.

I wanted to argue, but I felt woozy. Either that, or the smiley-face stickers on my ceiling could actually dance. Maybe closing my eyes for a second wouldn't hurt...

Before I knew it, Anthony had slipped the pill onto my tongue. I tried to spit it out, but it had already started to melt. Surprisingly, it tasted like caramel.

"Trust me, Jenny," I heard Jasmine say as everything started to fade. "You'll feel better when you wake up."

But I knew she was wrong. My bruises would heal, but I wouldn't feel better. Not tomorrow, and probably not ever.

PART II

PART II

Chapter Twenty-One

When I woke up, I was surprised to see Jasmine still sitting by my bedside. She was crocheting something that resembled a blue cockroach. I shuddered to think what it would look like as a piece of jewelry.

"Where's Anthony?" I said. My head felt heavier than a bowling ball, but the wooziness was gone.

"He went to fill Dr. Bradley in on how you were doing."

"How *am* I doing?'

"You should take it easy for a couple days, but you'll be all right." She looked up from her crocheting. "Oh, your aunt checked in on you a little while ago. I told her you'd sustained an injury during gym class."

I didn't *feel* all right. My insides ached like I'd been trying not to cry for hours. "Anthony should have let me stay in the Land of Tales. Maybe Ilda would have let me try the tasks again."

Jasmine leaned forward. Her face was full of pity, as if she felt sorry that I couldn't get the truth through my thick skull. "The mission is over, Jenny. They no longer want you there. Besides, what more can you do?"

"I don't know. *Something*. I can't just give up."

"You're not. You're being realistic. That's something every adventurer must learn eventually. You won't be able to save everyone."

"So I just let Ilda win?" I said.

She shook her head. "Don't think of it like that. You gave it a good try. What else were you supposed to do?"

Not fail. Not let myself get distracted. If only Ilda hadn't said all those things about my parents before I went off to do the third task, maybe I would have been able to keep my mind on climbing the glass mountain.

"I know you don't want to hear this, Jenny," said Jasmine, "but the Land of Tales doesn't want your help. You promised you'd leave if you couldn't complete the tasks, and you kept your word. So let the fairy-tale folks figure things out on their own, okay?"

She gave my shoulder a squeeze and headed for the door.

I hated to admit that Jasmine might be right. For the first time in my life, I'd been fired from a mission. Even if

140

I could find a way back to the Land of Tales, that wouldn't do any good.

I sighed and resisted the urge to hide under my covers.

Ilda's words started bouncing around in my head again. *Had* I been fooling myself in thinking I could find my parents? After all, I'd had no sign of my mom and dad, not even a clue, in seven years. Maybe that meant they weren't going to come back. Maybe that meant I needed to finally let them go.

A minute later, my bedroom door flew open, and Anthony and Dr. Bradley bustled in.

"Jenny!" the doctor said, hobbling over to me. "I'm so relieved you're all right."

"I'm fine," I said, ignoring the hollow feeling inside me.

Dr. Bradley shook his head thoughtfully. "Perhaps the Committee was right. Perhaps it was a mistake to send you to the Land of Tales when you had such personal ties to it."

I shrugged. "Maybe."

Anthony's mouth fell open. "Are you kidding? Who else were they going to send? You had to go, Jenny-girl. And now we have to find a way to get you back there so you can finish the job."

"They kicked me out, remember?"

"Forget that," said Anthony. "You need to get back to the Land of Tales before the seven years are up and Ilda gets total control over the kingdom. We can't let that crazy witch win."

"Anthony, I already told you that is impossible," said Dr. Bradley. "Princess Nartha has forbidden all adventurers from entering her land. If the Committee catches you breaking that rule, I'm afraid you might be out of a job."

"So that's it?" the gnome said, his cheeks flushed. "We're just supposed to give up? What about Ilda? What about Jenny's parents?"

Both of them looked at me with such sad eyes that I had to look away.

"I'm sorry," said Dr. Bradley. He gave my hand a gentle pat. "I'm afraid there's nothing more we can do."

My breath leaked out of me in a long sigh. This was it, I realized. This was the news I'd been dreading for seven years: hearing that my parents really were gone and that no one could bring them back. Knowing that there was no hope left.

I knew I should be focusing on a way to get rid of Ilda and help the Land of Tales, but I was too exhausted to even think about it. So I pushed Jack and Princess Nartha and everyone else as far into the back of my brain as I could, until they were practically in my ponytail. Then I looked Dr. Bradley in the face, and I forced myself to smile.

"You're right," I said. "We did what we could. It's time to move on."

After all, I had my friends; I had my aunt; and I had my life. That would have to be good enough.

Chapter Twenty-Two

I woke up the next morning to the sound of urgent squeaking. At first I thought one of my aunt's patients had wandered into my room. Then I realized the sound was coming from my adventuring bag.

"Oh, no!" I said, rushing to open it. Princess Aletha's mouse was curled up in a terrified little ball in the corner of the bag. I couldn't believe I'd forgotten all about him. "I'm so sorry, little guy."

I lifted Leonard out and petted his soft, pink head. Then I put him in an empty tissue box and promised to return with food and water. The mouse nodded like he understood. I wasn't normally a rodent fan, but a magical mouse didn't seem so bad.

Granted, once the magic in the Land of Tales disappeared for good tomorrow, Leonard would be nothing special. Even now, his fur was looking less bright pink than before. But until he lost all his magic, I could treat him as if he wasn't completely gross.

When I came back a minute later with a saucer full of water and a small hunk of cheese, Leonard practically threw himself on top of the food.

I couldn't believe that I'd not only let Aletha and her kingdom down, but I'd also accidentally kidnapped (and almost starved) her mouse. Judging by the dirty looks he was giving me as he gobbled one bite of cheese after another, Leonard wasn't too thrilled about the turn of events either.

It was time to get ready for school, but I hesitated about leaving Leonard behind. One of Aunt Evie's newest patients was a cat with an appetite-control problem. It would be cruel to leave Leonard at home with that kind of creature.

"How would you like to come to school with me?" I asked the mouse.

He seemed to shrug his shoulders, as if he wouldn't mind. Bringing a magical mouse to school didn't fit with my goal of having a normal life outside of adventuring, but I had to admit it would be nice to have the company.

Maybe then I wouldn't go through the entire day feeling crushingly lonely.

• • •

When I got to school (with Leonard safely tucked in a pocket of my backpack) I expected Trish and Melissa to give me the silent treatment after the fight we'd had. Instead, Melissa waved me over the minute I got off the bus.

"You're back," Trish said as the three of us went inside the school. "How was it?"

"Fine," I answered, even though that was far from the truth. I turned to Melissa. "How are you feeling?"

"I'm all healed!" As if to prove it, she made an eyes-bugging-out gesture as a cute guy from our science class walked by.

"So, you finished the three tasks?" said Trish, stopping at her locker. Instead of opening it, she stared at me like I was a combination she was trying to unlock.

I looked at my feet. "Not exactly." I didn't want to admit that I'd failed the mission. Maybe if I'd let my friends stay and help, things would have gone differently. But that didn't matter anymore, I told myself. I had put the Land of Tales far behind me.

"Can you not talk about it?" said Melissa, lowering her voice to a dramatic whisper. "Is it a secret or something?"

"Um, yeah," I found myself saying. "I probably shouldn't."

Trish and Melissa exchanged a look. "What about your parents?" said Trish. "Did you find any leads?"

I shook my head. "Nothing. The search is officially over."

"And you're okay with that?" said Melissa, her eyebrows raised.

"Yeah, I'm okay." Of course I wasn't. And I could tell I wasn't fooling anyone. But maybe if I pretended to be fine long enough, it would start to be true. Before my friends could ask any more questions, I added, "Are we still going to the dance tonight?"

"Are you kidding?" said Melissa. "I have my outfit all planned out!"

"Maybe we could go shopping after school for something I can wear," I suggested.

"Shopping?" Trish repeated. "I thought you hated that kind of stuff."

I shrugged. "Maybe I'll give it another chance." That's what regular girls did, after all. They went to dances, hung out with their friends, and did homework. Even if I didn't have a normal family or a normal life, that didn't mean I couldn't do normal activities like everyone else.

And besides, the more I filled up my days, the less time I'd have to think about what was missing.

. . .

Aunt Evie looked ready to burst with joy when I told her I was going over to Melissa's house to get ready for the dance.

"How exciting!" she said, hugging a chinchilla to her chest. Then my aunt's face fell a little. "But I did just get a call from your guidance counselor this morning about your grades."

"My grades?" I said.

"They've been slipping the past few weeks." Her brow furrowed. "Oh my, I wonder if that means I should ground you."

I couldn't believe it. My aunt had never grounded me. In fact, she'd never punished me at all. Why would she start now? Then again, until a few weeks ago, I'd always had Anthony to magically help me with my grades. Balancing adventuring and schoolwork all on my own was harder than I'd expected.

"It won't happen again," I said. "I promise. I'll start doing better in school."

Aunt Evie didn't look convinced. "Perhaps if I don't allow you to go to the dance, you'll learn your lesson."

Suddenly, blazing anger flared up in my gut. "No!" I said. "I have to go to the dance. It's my first one! You can't just take that away from me."

"I'm afraid I can, kitten. I am your guardian, and I have the right to —"

"No way!" I said. "You can't punish me like that. You're not my mom!"

Then I grabbed my bag and bolted out of the house. It only took two steps before I started feeling horrible about what I'd said, but it was too late to turn back.

Chapter Twenty-Three

The dance was nothing like I'd expected it to be. On TV, school dances were always well-lit and attended by only about fifty kids. But this dance was dark and hot and crowded. The cafeteria windows were steamed up from all the body heat trapped inside. It felt like dancing in a sauna.

"Isn't this fun?" Melissa yelled as she jumped around to a song I'd never heard before. Even Trish was dancing, which I'd never thought possible. She was doing something that looked like it was supposed to be the robot, but reminded me of a possessed puppet.

I checked that Leonard was safely tucked away in my purse. Then I closed my eyes and let the pumping music wash over me as I bopped around, waving my arms like a flailing octopus. This was what doing normal things felt like, instead of spending all my time thinking about adventures and my missing parents. Maybe I could get used to this.

When a slow song came on and Eddie from my home-room came up and asked me to dance, I just gaped at him in shock for a minute. Then I nodded and we started sway-ing to the cheesy music.

Here I was, just an average girl dancing with an average boy—one who wasn't secretly a barnyard animal. I glanced over at Melissa and Trish, who were grinning at me like proud parents.

Then I heard Eddie gasp as something skittered onto my shoulder. Uh-oh.

Sure enough, Leonard had gotten tired of hiding away in my purse and was out exploring. He ran down my arm and jumped onto Eddie's hand.

"It's okay," I said as Eddie's eyes doubled in size. "It's just a mouse. He won't hurt you."

But Leonard seemed determined to prove me wrong as he lifted his tail. A second later, there was a small puddle on the palm of Eddie's hand.

Eddie stared at the scene for a long second. Then he shrieked like a little girl and flung Leonard onto the floor. "Mouse pee!" he yelled. "Mouse pee!"

The clearly terrified mouse started to flee across the dance floor. "What is that?" I heard someone shriek.

Leonard's pink fur was so faded that it looked almost gray, but it was still no color a regular mouse should be.

I took off after the mouse at full speed, following the trail of people's surprised cries. Even some teachers let out bloodcurdling screams. I prayed Leonard didn't panic and run up someone's leg.

Finally, I caught sight of him as he slipped right under the door of the boys' bathroom. Great.

After a moment of hesitation, I threw open the door and ran after him.

"Attention!" I yelled in my most authoritative voice. "Emergency Bathroom Situation, Code 55667. I need you all to leave immediately!"

A few pairs of boys' feet scampered past me as I scanned the bathroom floor. "Leonard?" I said softly. "It's okay. You're safe now."

Finally, I saw a dash of pink in the corner. Ignoring the smelliness and general grossness of the bathroom, I knelt on the tile floor and put out my hand. Trembling, Leonard climbed into my palm.

I rubbed his velvety ears and then gently put him back into my purse.

"Jenny?" I heard Trish calling from the other side of the

door. When I got out into the hallway, my friends were looking at me like I was a mental patient.

"Are you okay?" said Melissa. "What happened? Was that the mouse Aletha gave you?"

I nodded. "I kind of stole him by accident. I figured bringing him with me would be safer than leaving him at home, but I guess I totally ruined the dance, huh?"

"You didn't ruin it," said Trish.

"Tell that to Eddie," I said as I spotted him running out of the cafeteria, holding his hand out like it was on fire. He'd probably never ask a girl to dance again.

"He'll get over it," said Trish. "People are already laughing about the whole thing. They think someone let a dyed hamster loose in here."

"Yeah, no big deal," said Melissa. "You want to go dance again?"

I shook my head. Suddenly, I felt exhausted. "I think I'll just go home."

"What?" said Melissa. "But you just got here. And we're having fun!"

"I know, but I don't really feel like dealing with any more mouse escapes."

Melissa and Trish exchanged a look. "Come on, Jenny,"

said Trish. "You don't have to pretend with us. We know why you're really upset."

"What are you talking about?"

"Your parents, silly," said Melissa. "Now that you lost their trail, it's totally normal to be bummed about it."

"I'm not bummed. I'm fine."

Trish put her hand on my arm. "You keep saying that, but I don't think it's true. I think you're just fooling yourself."

I shook her off. "I told you, I'm okay. And I don't want to talk about this anymore."

Before my friends could say anything else, I rushed past them and headed for the door. I couldn't believe it. How many times were they going to bring this up? I'd finally learned to let my parents go. Why couldn't they do the same?

• • •

When I got home, I sat on my bed staring at my mother's bracelet. I hadn't taken it off in weeks, but for some reason it now felt heavy and itchy around my wrist. Finally, I undid the clasp and pulled it off. The purple gems sparkled at me as usual, but this time the sight of them wasn't comforting; it just made me sad. And I was tired of being sad. I was tired of missing my parents. I was tired of aching because they were gone.

On a whim, I grabbed my jewelry box and slipped the bracelet inside. Then I pulled out a photo album I kept tucked under my nightstand and opened it. I hadn't let myself look at the photos in a long time.

The first few pages were filled with baby pictures of me. I wished I could say I'd been a cute baby, but really I'd looked a lot like a little old man with a squished face and patchy hair. In fact, the baby version of me could have passed for Princess Nartha's ancient servant.

When I was a few pages in, the photo album suddenly felt heavy in my hands. I stared down at a picture of my parents and me having a picnic under a huge maple tree. Three-year-old me was curled up in my dad's lap with a tinfoil crown on my head, while my mom laughingly threw a flower at whoever was taking the picture. The three of us looked so happy, like a real family.

As I leaned in closer, the necklace my mom was wearing caught my eye. It was a silver chain with a handful of purple gems dangling from it. The gems were identical to the ones in my bracelet. The two pieces of jewelry must have been a set.

Somehow I hadn't noticed that necklace before. It definitely wasn't in the jewelry box I'd inherited from my mom. Could that mean she'd had the necklace on the day she'd disappeared?

All this time, I'd been wearing the bracelet and not realizing that wherever my mom was, she could have a matching piece of jewelry around her neck.

But what good was thinking about things like that?

I slammed the photo album shut and put it in my closet. Then I went around my room, gathering up all the things that reminded me of my parents: a tattered book of fairy tales they'd given me for my fifth birthday, a stuffed bear so flattened that it looked more like an otter, the yarn Indiana Jones whip my mother had made me for Halloween one year. I put all these things way in the back of my closet behind my mini-golf equipment. Then I firmly shut the door.

Chapter Twenty-Four

In the morning, I checked on Leonard to make sure he was okay in his tissue-box nest. He was even grayer than the day before, but otherwise he looked fine. When I talked to him, he just stared at me like a regular mouse would. Clearly, his ability to understand human speech was almost gone. By tonight, he'd be just an average mouse.

I didn't let myself think about what that meant for the Land of Tales. They'd be fine without magic. They'd have no choice but to get used to it. And to Ilda.

Clearly, I wasn't doing a good job of *not* thinking about things. I tapped my forehead to try to dislodge some of those pesky thoughts.

When I went downstairs, I found Aunt Evie rolling out dough on the kitchen table. To the untrained eye, it would have looked like cookie dough, but I knew it would eventually become ostrich treats for one of her newest patients.

I tried to tune out the angry squawks coming from the basement as I made myself some toast.

My aunt barely glanced in my direction. She obviously was still upset about how I'd yelled at her the night before.

"Aunt Evie?"

"Mm?"

"I'm sorry about what I said yesterday. You're not my mom, but you're the only family I have. And…and you're right about my grades. I'll work on them, okay?"

My aunt nodded and smiled. "I know it's hard for you without your parents, dear. I can't even imagine how you must feel."

She looked at me expectantly, but I didn't know what to say. The last thing I wanted to do was talk about my parents for the millionth time. But what I'd said to my aunt was true: she was my only family and the closest thing I had to a parent. Maybe it was time I started thinking of her that way.

"How about we do something fun today?" I asked. "Just the two of us?"

My aunt blinked at me. "What would you like to do?"

I smiled, realizing there was one activity my aunt was bound to enjoy.

• • •

158

The mini-golf course was pirate-themed, complete with a miniature pirate ship. Aunt Evie looked nervous as I dragged her onto the course. She was completely out of her element holding a mini-golf club instead of a cup of tea, and without an animal or two hanging on her. But she smiled and looked willing to give it a shot.

After trying to hit the ball with the handle of the club a couple of times, Aunt Evie finally got the hang of things. I tried not to get too low of a score so she wouldn't get discouraged. By the time we were halfway through the course, my aunt and I were chatting and laughing as if our fight had never happened. I couldn't remember the last time we'd had so much fun together.

But just as we were getting to the last hole—a giant clown face that made me shiver—Leonard started squeaking in my bag. Aunt Evie gave me a strange look.

"Are you all right, dear?" she said. "Is that you whimpering?"

I plastered a fake smile on my face. "Nope. I'm fine."

But I could tell she could see right through my pretend cheerfulness. "What is it? What's the matter?"

I shook my head, wishing I could tell her about what was going on, and about poor Leonard and how I'd failed him. Not only was it against the rules for me to tell my aunt about being an adventurer, but she probably wouldn't know how to handle the truth.

When I didn't say anything, Aunt Evie's face softened. "Is it your parents, dear? I noticed you stopped wearing your mother's bracelet."

A wave of anger erupted inside me. Did I have an "ask me about my parents" sign taped to my back?

"No!" I cried. "It has nothing to do with them, okay? Why can't everyone just leave me alone?"

I stomped off to finish our mini-golf game. I swung the club and got the ball right into the clown's mouth. Hole-in-one. But instead of celebrating, I felt like crying. What was wrong with me?

"Jenny," Aunt Evie said. "Come here." She led me to a bench and sat me down. "Did I ever tell you about the morning your parents left, before they disappeared?"

I shook my head. My aunt hardly ever talked about my parents, and she avoided mentioning anything about that day.

"Why?" I said. "What happened?"

Aunt Evie chewed on her lip. "Your mom and dad brought you over like they usually did when they went away on business. They said they'd be back in a couple days, but two days went by, and there was no sign of them. Then three days. By then I got worried and called the police. It turned out there was no record of the dentistry convention they were supposed to be attending. That's when the police officially declared them missing."

"Why are you telling me this?" I said. It wasn't making me feel any better.

My aunt sighed. "The thing is, dear, it occurred to me afterward that they had both been acting a little strangely that day. Your mother insisted on saying good-bye to you again, after she'd already put you to bed, like she knew she would be gone for longer than a couple days. And I...well, I don't think my brother would like me saying this...but he seemed a little afraid."

"Afraid? Of what?"

"I have no idea." She looked up at me. "But the important thing is that they went, even though they were clearly anxious about something. Your parents were always like that. Like the time my brother helped me hypnotize an elephant, even though he was allergic to its ear hair. He forged ahead even when it was difficult and he couldn't stop sneezing."

I finally understood what my aunt was saying. "And

161

that's what we have to do, right? Go on without my mom and dad even though it's hard?"

My aunt nodded. "And it *is* hard, isn't it? Sometimes, I want more than anything for them to come back so we can all be a family again."

Our conversation sent my brain spinning. If my parents had been unusually nervous before the mission, they must have known they were up against something big. But what? Were they afraid of Ilda? Or of something else?

And yet they'd gone on the mission anyway. Even though they were afraid, even though they knew they might not see me again, they'd still gone.

Because that's what adventurers did. They didn't learn how to pick their battles like Jasmine claimed. If they knew something had to be done, they did it, no matter what. Not because there was something in it for them, but because other people needed their help.

I realized I'd gone to the Land of Tales for all the wrong reasons. I hadn't really cared about helping the kingdom. I'd been far too focused on finding my parents. No wonder I'd messed everything up.

And that was why I had to go back.

Chapter Twenty-Five

"You want us to *what*?" said Melissa when the three of us were gathered in my room that afternoon.

"Help me trick Anthony again so I can go back to the Land of Tales," I repeated. "And it has to be today, before it's too late."

"But I don't understand," said Trish. "You already went there and saved the day. Why do you have to go back?"

I sighed. It was time to fess up. "Because I screwed up. I failed the last task. You guys were right. I couldn't do it without your help."

I stopped, realizing that what I'd said was true. Maybe having my friends along hadn't been perfect, but who knows how far I would have gotten without them? I might have failed the first task like everyone else except Sir Knight.

"I'm sorry for how I treated you guys," I went on. "I just got scared that something would happen to you. I could never forgive myself if you got really hurt because of me. But I did need your help then—and I definitely need it now. Can you forgive me for being a jerk?"

Trish and Melissa looked at each other. Then Melissa grinned and started singing:

> *We forgive you,*
> *You silly horseshoe.*
> *You're a good friend, girl,*
> *Though your hair will not curl.*

This time I wanted to laugh not because the song was awful (which, let's face it, it was), but because I was so glad that everything was okay with us again.

"So where do we start?" said Trish after Melissa was (mercifully) done singing.

"Well, you managed to trick Anthony once," I said. "We need to figure out a way to do it again."

"Why won't he just take you without us tricking him?" said Trish.

"Because adventurers aren't allowed in the Land of Tales anymore. Even Anthony wouldn't break a rule like that on purpose. He can't risk losing his job. But if he doesn't realize he's doing it, maybe he won't get in trouble."

Trish scrunched her eyebrows together. "What if he didn't bring you back?" she said slowly. "What if he only brought *us*?"

"No way," I said. "I'm not going to let you guys go back there without me."

"I know," said Trish. "I just mean, what if Anthony brings us there, not realizing he's bringing you along, too?"

"But how would that work?" said Melissa. "We can't shrink Jenny and put her in one of our backpacks." She wrinkled her forehead. "Can we?"

"We won't need to," said Trish, her smile getting bigger by the second. "I've got a plan."

• • •

The first step to making Trish's plan work was to head to the candy store in town. The shop reminded me a lot of Ilda's house: the roof was brick red and the walls were decorated to look like gingerbread. Luckily, the store clerk accepted money as payment instead of humiliation.

As Melissa, Trish, and I huddled behind some bushes across the street, Trish filled me in on how they'd managed to bribe Anthony the first time.

"Melissa and I ran into him at the candy store, right after he went on his diet."

"He was drooling so much, there was a puddle on the floor!" said Melissa.

Trish grinned. "We barely had to say the word 'candy' and he was willing to take us to the moon."

"Look!" Melissa said, jabbing me in the ribs. I was starting to think I should get her elbow pads for her birthday. "There he is! I told you he'd come back at his usual time."

Anthony was moseying on down the street, chewing on some broccoli with a pained look on his face. He wore a nondescript coat over his brightly colored clothes and a hat pulled low over his flaming hair. He was still shorter than almost everyone else on the street, but otherwise he blended in surprisingly well.

"Ready?" Trish asked me.

I nodded and crossed my fingers that this plan worked. Otherwise, I had no idea what I'd do. Then I checked on Leonard who was tucked into the corner of my bag. Hopefully, I'd be able to get him safely back home.

"Anthony!" Melissa called as she hurried down the street, waving. The gnome stopped.

I watched them talking for a minute. Then I saw Melissa

pull a bag of candy out of her pocket. Anthony's eyes practically fell out of his head. When Melissa offered him a piece, he gobbled it up and looked desperate for more.

I started to creep along the street, hiding behind benches so Anthony wouldn't see me. Just as I crouched near a mailbox, Trish hurried down the street past me.

"Melissa!" she said. "I'm so glad I found you. Have you seen my notebook? The one with all my magic notes in it?"

"No," said Melissa. "When was the last time you saw it?"

Trish pretended to think for a minute. Then she gasped. "I must have dropped it when we were on that adventure with Jenny. Probably when you got injured in the lake. It must still be there."

Melissa turned to Anthony. "Do you think you could take us back to look for it?"

Anthony shook his head. "Sorry, no can do."

"But I need those notes or I'll flunk out of school!" Trish said with a wail. "I'll die! Please!" She grabbed Anthony's arm and started fake-sobbing into his shoulder.

If there was one thing Anthony couldn't stand, it was crying. "Now, now. It's okay. Maybe I could go find the notebook for you."

"But you don't know what it looks like!" said Trish

through her imaginary tears, putting on an impressive performance. "And what if that monster eats you while you're looking for it? You need someone to keep an eye out."

"Monster?" said Anthony. "The one that tried to strangle Melissa?"

Melissa nodded. "My ribs still hurt a little, but I guess that's what happens when a creature squeezes you so hard that you pass out. And almost die." She smiled brightly. "I'm sure that wouldn't happen to you, though."

I could practically hear Anthony gulp.

"Well, maybe I could…" Anthony took off his hat and put it back on again. "I mean, you two aren't adventurers, so it might be okay…" He still didn't look convinced.

"We'll pay you!" said Melissa. "Anything you want."

"Anything I want?" he said, his eyes wandering over to the candy-store's window display. After his taste of sugar, he was clearly willing to do whatever it took to get more.

I couldn't help smiling. Ding! Ding! Ding! We'd won.

After Trish had promised Anthony all the candy he could eat, I waited until Anthony, Trish, and Melissa went around the side of the building where they could safely disappear. Then I crept to the corner and waited. Just as I heard the *Pop!* I lunged forward and grabbed on to Trish's backpack.

The four of us spun in between worlds before being spit out near the edge of Nessie's lake. The minute we arrived, I let go of Trish and jumped behind a bush before Anthony noticed me.

As my friends led Anthony around the lake, pretending to look for the notebook, I snuck away toward the woods. I glanced over my shoulder and saw Trish looking at me with a smile on her face.

"Thank you," I mouthed.

She gave me a small wave before turning back to Anthony. Something told me she was going to write the best English paper anyone had ever read.

I was swimming in warm, fuzzy feelings as I hurried through the forest. My friends were the best. I was never going to take them for granted again.

Chapter Twenty-Six

My first stop would be Ilda's house. I had to convince her to let me try the third task one more time. Otherwise, sneaking back into the Land of Tales would be all for nothing.

On the way, I spotted Jack Beanstalk doing stretches near his farm. This time, his brothers were nowhere in sight.

"You're back!" he said, rushing over to me. "They said you deserted us."

"Of course not. I promised I'd help, and I'm going to."

Jack looked at me doubtfully. "But you only have until sunset today. Do you really think you can do it?"

"The curse ends at sunset?" I'd assumed I'd have until midnight.

"And the festival's starting soon. My brothers have already gone ahead." Jack sighed. "I hope my tail disappears right away this time. Last year, it took days for it to fade. My oldest brother's nose still looks more piggish than it did before."

"I guess I'd better hurry," I said.

Jack flashed me a smile. "Good luck. I hope you don't fail!"

"Um, thanks." Me too.

• • •

When I got to Ilda's house, I took a deep breath and knocked on the door. Almost instantly, the witch's smiling face appeared in the doorway. Today she was wearing her best ensemble yet: a pair of shamrock earrings and a purple cardigan covered with glittery rainbows. I knew some unicorns who would love the sight of her. If only I could get them to come and stick her with their horns.

"Oh, you're back," she said. "I thought they'd driven you out of this land."

"I'm not that easy to get rid of," I said.

Ilda laughed, flashing her lipstick-stained teeth. "Perseverance is a virtue!"

"I want you to let me try the third task again," I said.

She shook her head, her smile fading. "I'm afraid that's impossible. Everyone gets one chance, and that's it. Now if you'll excuse me, I have a festival to get to."

Ilda tried to push past me, but I blocked her way. "If you're so sure the tasks are impossible, what's the harm in letting me try?"

"Because those are the rules. They wouldn't like it if…" She broke off, wincing like she'd said too much.

"Who wouldn't like it?" I said.

The witch let out a high-pitched giggle. "The other people who've already attempted the tasks, of course. It wouldn't be fair to them, would it?"

Since when did Ilda care about fairness?

This time she did manage to push past me and out of the house. She clapped her hands loudly and waited, but nothing happened. Then she snapped her fingers, stomped her feet, and flapped her arms in an elaborate crazy chicken dance. Still nothing.

"Where is that rooster?" she said, throwing her hands up in frustration. "Some creatures are just hopeless, no matter how much you teach them."

My mind was spinning. Everyone had a price: Anthony's candy bribe proved that. I just had to figure out what Ilda's weakness was.

And then it came to me: Humiliation. That's what she loved the most.

"Okay, you like to make deals, right? How about this: You let me redo the last task during the festival today."

Ilda's mouth curled up in amusement. "And why would I do that?"

"Think about it. Me failing in front of everyone will be like the crowning jewel of the event. And when it's all done, the land's magic will be gone, I'll be a pancake, and you'll have won."

Ilda played with the chain around her neck as she thought over what I'd said. The fact that she was considering it at all was a good sign.

"That's a start," she said. "But I'm not sure that would teach you enough of a lesson. How about this? *When* you fail, if you're still alive, you will voluntarily allow me to turn you into any type of object I want. Maybe a rock or a bush or a wheel of cheese. That way I can use you as an example and everyone will benefit!"

What could I say? I wasn't thrilled about the idea of spending the rest of my life as a hunk of stinky cheese, but I didn't have a choice. I would just have to make sure not to fail this time.

"Fine," I said. "But if I succeed, you have to give the land its magic back and reverse all the curses you've put on everyone. And after that, you'll leave this land alone forever."

"Very well," said Ilda, her voice sweet and sticky. She obviously thought I was a fool for making this deal with her. "Your humiliation will be the star attraction of the festival." She giggled. "Then everyone will be able to learn from your failure! If only your parents had—"

I made myself tune out her words as I stomped away. Nothing was going to distract me from succeeding this time.

Chapter Twenty-Seven

As I made my way toward the glass mountain, I passed dozens of people getting ready for the festival. The vibe in the village was somber and resigned, as if everyone had given up. I couldn't say I blamed them. If I lived in this place, I'd probably feel defeated too. Ilda seemed to feed off everyone's crushed hopes.

When I got to the mountain, the sun was high in the sky, which meant that the festival had already started. This time, as I got ready to climb, I was a little more prepared. I pulled a length of rope out of my bag and tied it around my waist. Then I looped the extra rope at my hip, hoping it would be long enough to make my plan work.

After stretching out my fingers and ignoring the aches and pains from the last time I'd attempted this crazy task, I got to work. This time, climbing was much easier, mostly because my mind was on what I was doing. Everything else faded away until I was just focused on finding one foothold after the next.

Within a few minutes, I reached the same ledge I'd fallen off the first time. I glanced up at the perfectly smooth rock face above me. I'd gone as far as I could go. Now all I could do was wait.

And wait.

And wait.

The sun was starting to get lower in the sky, which made my stomach clench. I was running out of time. What if this didn't work?

I found myself composing little rhymes in my head to pass the time, ones that were about ten times worse than anything Melissa had ever written. Next time I heard one of her songs, I'd try not to be so judgmental. *If* I ever saw her again, that is.

As I pushed that thought out of my head, I heard a sound from below. The last thing I wanted to do was look down, but I couldn't help myself. A crowd of villagers was coming toward the mountain. They were covered in mud and some of them still had animal parts: a horse's tail, a donkey head. No doubt Ilda had sent them here so they could see me mess up.

A minute later, Ilda rode up on the Monsterooster. Sure enough, she had dressed it up in a bonnet that perfectly matched her sparkly purple sweater. The witch looked completely ridiculous and yet totally in control. She started ordering people to set up a stage, probably so she could have everyone watch as she turned me into a hunk of cheddar later.

Seeing how miserable the villagers looked, how filthy and defeated, made determination sweep through my whole body. Ilda expected me to fail, but I'd promised these people I would help them. And that was exactly what I was going to do.

Finally, my ears picked up the sound I'd been waiting for: *Skree! Skree! Skree!*

I'd never thought I'd be glad to see a murderous bird charging at me, but it was all part of my plan. My crazy, potentially suicidal plan.

I grabbed the rope and held the loose end up like a lasso. As the bird drew nearer, suddenly I heard another sound coming from below: *Clang. Clang! CLANG!*

"Fair maiden, do not fear!" I heard Sir Knight call. "I'm coming to rescue you."

Perfect. Just what I needed.

"No!" I cried, as the clanging drew closer. "I don't want your help. Turn back!"

But he wouldn't listen to me. Either that, or he couldn't hear me over the sound of his ridiculously loud armor.

I tried to forget about the knight and focus on the task at hand. The bird drew closer and closer. As it swooped at me, I tossed the lasso into the air and—success! The rope wrapped around the bird's neck. The beast shrieked and started to pull up. Since the other end of the rope was tightly fastened around my waist, the bird couldn't go anywhere without taking me with it.

For a second, I was flying! And then—

Clang!

Sir Knight grabbed on to my leg. "Do not fear, maiden! I'll protect you."

"Let go of me!" I yelled as the bird flapped its giant black wings, straining to rise into the air. The knight was ruining everything. I tried to free my leg, but he held on tight.

Slowly, the bird managed to climb upward with me dangling from its neck and Sir Knight dangling from my leg. Boy, was he heavy. I felt like I was being dragged down by a boulder filled with boulders.

"Hold on, maiden!" Sir Knight called.

"*You* hold on," I said, since we were too high up now for him to safely jump down. "I have a plan. Just stay out of the way!"

We got higher and higher, gliding along the gleaming mountain. I tried not to look down, and I tried to ignore the distinctly oily smell coming off the bird's feathers.

As the ground started to feel seriously far away, I closed my eyes, hoping I was right and the bird would take me to the top of the mountain. Fingers crossed that today wasn't the day the bird decided to keep going into the clouds to see what was beyond them. I hadn't remembered to pack my spacesuit.

Finally, just as I'd hoped, we reached the mountain peak and the bird started to skim along it. The glass here was so thin and sharp that it looked like it could easily slice me in half. I didn't know how there could be a magical object up here—wouldn't it have slid off?—but I grabbed a knife out of my bag and got ready to slice through the rope at the first sight of anything that looked promising.

We hadn't gone far before the bird suddenly dove again. As we lurched forward, the rope cut into my waist, making me gasp for air. I glanced down to check how Sir Knight was doing—just in time to see him lose his grip on my leg and drop like a hunk of metal.

Chapter Twenty-Eight

"No!" I yelled as the weight on my leg disappeared.

I strained to look down, expecting to hear Sir Knight's armor hit the mountain. But instead, I heard something else. Squawking.

What the—?

As we got lower, the source of the squawking appeared. Directly below me—perched along the very tippy-top of the mountain—was a huge nest with several couch-sized baby birds snuggled inside. The chorus of chirps was louder than a marching band.

I needed a second to spot Sir Knight in the middle of the feathery chaos. The birds had him pinned down, clearly thinking dinner had arrived. Luckily, their beaks bounced right off his armor. *Ping. Ping. Ping.*

The knight might have been all right for the moment, but how was I going to get him out of there?

As the mama bird got lower, I saw Sir Knight manage to scramble to his feet.

"Maiden!" he called over the nearly deafening chirps. "Are you all right?"

I had to hand it to the knight. Even when his life was in danger, he still made sure the damsel he was "saving" was all in one piece.

"I'm fine!" I called. "Don't move."

He said something back, but at that moment the mama bird let out another ear-piercing *skree*! In response, the baby birds started chirping back even louder. I was afraid my ears might pop from the noise.

Sir Knight was still trying to tell me something, but it was no use. Finally, he started waving his arms, and that's when I realized he was holding some sort of object.

A gleaming goblet.

I stared at it like it was made of gold...which it was. That had to be the object Ilda wanted me to find. Why else would a goblet be at the top of a mountain?

"Don't move!" I yelled. "I'll get you out!" If Sir Knight tried to climb out of the nest on his own, there was a good chance he'd just go tumbling down the mountain.

The mama bird was about to land in the nest, and I

knew we were running out of time. If the knight and I were underneath her when she landed, we'd be crushed. My only hope was that we could steer the mama bird back down the mountain somehow.

"Sir Knight!" I called. "The minute you can reach my leg, grab on!" I mimed the action, just in case he still couldn't hear me.

After a minute, he waved, which I hoped meant my message had gotten through. He crouched like he was getting ready to jump, while still batting the hungry birds away.

The mama bird flapped her wings as she prepared to swoop into the nest, and I was finally low enough for the knight to jump up and grab on to my leg again.

I waited for him to jump, but nothing happened.

"Jump!" I yelled.

He was yelling something back. I strained to hear and finally made out one word: "Jump!"

Wait, was he trying to get me to jump down into the bird nest? That was crazy! Then we'd both be stuck. And unlike him, I didn't have full-body armor to keep me from becoming bird food. I'd just have to hope I wasn't delicious.

"No, *you* jump!" I tried to mime with my free hand while still holding on to the rope.

The knight gestured wildly as the bird got lower and lower. She circled, probably trying to figure out what to do about the very shiny new bird that had suddenly appeared in her nest.

"Jump now!" I cried.

Finally, the knight appeared to get the hint. He worked his way over to the edge of the nest and waited for the mama bird to swoop past. Then he crouched and jumped—

Only to trip and fall right out of the nest.

"Sir Knight!" I cried as I heard him hit the mountain slope. *Crash!*

Without thinking, I grabbed my knife and sliced through the rope keeping me tethered to the mama bird.

For a second, I just free fell, and that second was more than long enough for me to realize what a stupid thing I'd just done. Instead of climbing on the mama bird's back or finding some other way to control her so I could rescue the knight, now I was going to plummet to my death along with him. Anthony would never let me hear the end of it.

Then my knee slammed into something, and an instant later, my entire body hit the side of the mountain. I started to slide along the glass like a squeegee. I was alive!

Below me, I heard Sir Knight's armor scraping the side

of the mountain. I couldn't see if he was all right, but I prayed that he was all in one piece.

As I kept sliding down the mountain, I started going faster and faster. At this rate, I'd go splat when I hit the ground. I had to figure out some way to slow down. But everything was happening so fast, and I was totally out of ideas.

Suddenly, something shiny came into view below me. It was Sir Knight! Before I could call out his name, I slid right past him, and—

"Ugh!" I cried as something yanked me up by the back of my shirt.

"Hold still, maiden," I heard Sir Knight say. "I have you."

I craned my neck and realized Sir Knight was holding on to my shirt with one hand and hanging on to his sword with the other. Somehow, he'd managed to embed his sword in the side of the mountain.

When I glanced down, I saw that we were only a few feet above a ledge that was wide enough to stand on. If Sir Knight hadn't caught me and I'd kept going at top speed, I would have smacked right into it. *Ouch.*

"I will lower you down to the ledge," the knight said. "Then I will follow behind you."

"Okay," I called. I felt myself slipping lower and lower until my feet were almost at the ledge. "You can let go now."

I dropped down, just managing to catch my balance to keep from sailing over the side. Then I inched along the mountain to give the knight room to land. A minute later—*Crash!*—he came down on the ledge beside me.

"Are you all right, maiden?" he said, flipping up his helmet. *Ding!*

"Yeah, I'm fine. Thank you. You—" I almost laughed. "You saved my life." Those were definitely not words I thought I would ever say to Sir Knight, but they were true. Maybe he wasn't a total joke after all.

The knight shrugged. "All in a day's work, my lady. Now, I shall climb down the mountain. Then you may jump, and I shall catch you in my arms."

"Um, that's okay. I think I'd rather just climb down, too." Sir Knight had redeemed himself by catching me once, but I wasn't crazy enough to let him try it again.

The knight looked a little offended, but he didn't argue.

Finally, after what felt like an hour of climbing backward, the ground mercifully appeared under my feet. I flopped onto the grass, feeling flattened and exhausted.

After a minute, Sir Knight climbed down too and came

to sit next to me. We'd ended up on the opposite side of the mountain from Ilda and the villagers.

"Are you all right?" I asked.

"Certainly," Sir Knight answered. "Why wouldn't I be?" I had a feeling that even if he'd been swallowed by a whale, the knight would have still claimed to be fine.

"Any chance you still have the goblet?" I asked, knowing it was a long shot.

Sir Knight's eyes widened. "Do you even have to ask, maiden? Of course I was able to rescue the goblet. I am a knight!" He pulled off his helmet and fished around inside. Then he held up the goblet in triumph.

I didn't bother asking how Sir Knight had managed to cram both his head and the goblet into the helmet at once. All I cared about was that he had the third magical object.

I could have cried with relief as I put the goblet into my bag alongside the spray bottle and the metal fly swatter. The sun was still a good way above the horizon, which meant I had plenty of time before the curse ended. Maybe I could really pull this thing off.

Chapter Twenty-Nine

After I managed to convince Sir Knight that I was okay to walk and didn't need to be carried—now *that* would be humiliating—we headed toward the stage on the other side of the mountain. In truth, my knee was aching from its collision with the glass mountain, but I ignored the pain. I'd have time for injuries later.

As we got to the stage Ilda had set up, we saw her announcing the winners (and losers) of the events. When she spotted me, all in one piece, her usual fake smile turned into a grimace.

"Ilda!" I said, pushing through the crowd toward the stage. Everyone fell quiet and stared at me as if they couldn't believe I was still alive. "I've completed your three tasks. Now you have to lift the curse."

As I rushed onto the stage, something like concern flickered across the witch's face. Then she laughed and said, "Nonsense. No one can complete the tasks."

"But I have." I glanced at Sir Knight who was standing behind me. "*We* have."

"Didn't anyone ever teach you it's wrong to lie?" she said, crossing her arms in front of her chest.

"I'm not lying. Look!" I opened my bag and held up the goblet. But something was wrong with it. Instead of shining as it had earlier, it was cracked and crumbling. In fact, it wasn't made out of gold at all. It was just plaster painted to look like gold.

"What is this?" said Ilda, grabbing the goblet from me. The minute her hand touched it, the plaster crumbled into pieces. "Are you trying to trick me?"

I stared at the pile of dust at my feet. "I don't understand. I completed the task. You wanted the object from the top of the mountain, and I brought it to you."

"You brought me a fake," said Ilda. She turned to the crowd. "Do you see what adventurers do? They cheat to get what they want. They don't care about people like you. They only care about glory."

The crowd turned to glare at me, all their previous suspicions back even stronger. People booed and hissed. I caught sight of Jack's thin face in the crowd. He looked heartbroken. I didn't care what the other villagers thought, but I couldn't stand the thought of him being disappointed in me.

"Lies!" said Sir Knight, stepping forward. "We retrieved the goblet together. It's the real thing."

I appreciated the knight's effort, especially since his trembling knees showed he was still afraid of the witch, but it was no use. He wasn't terribly popular with the people of the village, and I didn't think I could do or say anything to prove Ilda wrong. And that was, after all, what she wanted.

Suddenly, I realized how clueless I'd been.

"The tasks were a lie from the start, weren't they?" I said. "You never intended to give the kingdom its magic back. You just wanted to play a little game."

"How dare you accuse me of such a thing?" said Ilda, but I could see the amusement on her face. I was right. That had been her plan all along. The tasks were impossible because they were fake. Everything I'd done had been for nothing.

I marched over and stood face-to-face with the witch. "So that's it, then?" I said. "You're taking the last of the magic and there's no way to get it back?"

"Now, Jenny, don't be a sore loser. If you had completed the tasks—"

"Stop lying!" I yelled, feeling ready to burst. "I'm sick of your games. Just tell me the truth!"

Ilda stepped back, and for once she actually looked a little afraid. She grabbed at her necklace, and that's when I spotted them. The purple gems dangling from the silver chain. They'd been hidden under the witch's gaudy sweaters, but now I could see them clearly.

"Where did you get that?" I whispered.

Ilda blinked. "What do you mean?"

"The necklace. It was my mother's. Where did you get it?"

"Oh, this?" she said, pulling it out so I could see the string of purple gems that perfectly matched those still in my jewelry box at home. "It was a gift. Your mother gave it to me."

"Liar! She would never do that. Give it back!" I lunged forward and tried to grab the necklace, but Ilda managed to sidestep me.

Just then a mighty howl echoed from somewhere nearby. "*Arooo*!" Everyone froze, even me.

The howl came again, fierce and angry. I turned to see Ralph the wolf standing just past the crowd. A few feet behind him was the giant boulder he was cursed to always be attached to. Somehow, he'd managed to drag it all the way here.

His eyes looked almost red and there was froth around his mouth. At first I thought his narrowed eyes were focused on Ilda. Then I realized he was staring down the Monsterooster.

"Finally," Ralph snarled, "the beast will be mine."

Chapter Thirty

"What are you doing here, Wolf?" Ilda demanded.

"You thought you could keep me under control forever," said Ralph, inching closer. Each of his labored steps dragged the boulder along. The stunned crowd parted to let him through. "But seven years of exercise have finally paid off, and now I'm strong enough that your curse can't stop me."

The Monsterooster was completely frozen in terror at the foot of the stage. I didn't want to let Ilda out of my sight, but I had to do something. I couldn't let Ralph gobble up the helpless rooster in front of everyone. Or at all.

"Sir Knight," I said. "Can't you stop him?"

The knight shook his head. "Ralph has earned his revenge. We all have."

Clearly, I would get no help there. I turned back to Ralph. "You don't want to do this!" I called out.

"Oh yes, I do," Ralph said with a growl. Then he dropped to all fours and went straight for the Monsterooster's throat.

The rooster screeched and flapped his wings. At the same moment, Ilda grabbed her necklace and mumbled something under her breath. A bolt of lightning flew at Ralph, but the wolf managed to jump out of the way. Instead of hitting him, the lightning zapped the ground and sent huge sparks flying everywhere.

Ralph started to charge forward again. For some reason, the boulder behind him was no longer moving. He stopped running and whirled around. "The rope," he said in disbelief. "It's gone."

I realized that Ilda's lightning bolt must have broken the invisible rope that had kept Ralph attached to the boulder. He was free. Which was good news for Ralph, but really bad news for the rooster.

The wolf turned back toward us with a sneer on his long face. "Finally," he said. Then he crouched, ready to pounce. The rooster's eyes were bugging out so much that they looked like they might pop.

As I racked my brain for a plan, I noticed that the sun had officially set. Did that mean I was too late? Had time run out and all the land's magic was gone?

"Stand back, Wolf!" cried Ilda. "I will not have you eating my pet!"

She pushed me aside, and I stumbled forward. My bag fell off my shoulder and landed on the ground. Instantly, as if he'd just been waiting for his chance, Leonard jumped out of my bag and skittered away. He was running so fast that I couldn't even see his legs moving.

The mouse darted off the stage and ran right in front of the giant rooster's nose.

The Monsterooster's terrified eyes turned downright panicked. Apparently, the combination of a wolf and a mouse was just too much for him to handle.

The rooster reared his head, let out an ear-piercing squawk, and started fluttering his giant wings again. He was flapping them so furiously this time that his saddle started to slip off. After a moment, the saddle fell onto the dirt and the rooster started to lift off the ground. I was pretty sure that such an enormous bird taking flight defied the laws of nature, but the Monsterooster was obviously too terrified to care about physics.

Ralph charged after the bird but was too late. When he realized he couldn't reach the rooster, the wolf stood absolutely still, his jaw hanging open, watching his dinner fly away. Then he let out a long, pained howl. "Is this my punishment?" he cried at the heavens. "I'm sorry I ever ate that red riding girl!" Then he turned and retreated into the woods, his tail between his legs.

"Where are you going, my pet? Come back!" Ilda shrieked toward the sky, but the rooster wasn't listening. It was turning into a smaller and smaller speck among the clouds.

The witch craned her neck and did her crazy chicken dance, but it didn't help. Finally, she clasped the necklace and mumbled something under her breath. Her eyes widened, and her words got louder. I realized what was happening: she was trying to cast a spell, but it wasn't working.

Ilda screamed in frustration and tore off the necklace. Her face grew so red that it looked like a giant apple. "They betrayed me! They told me I'd still have my magic, and now it's gone!" Her eyes swung to where the sun had just set behind the trees. "It's over. They took all the magic for themselves, and they betrayed me."

"What do you mean?" I said. "Who betrayed you?"

Her eyes were wild like a trapped animal's. "What am I supposed to do without my power? They promised me. They said if I just waited seven years and let them drain the magic from the land, I could keep my own. They said this necklace would give me magic forever and that I could finally have my revenge."

"Revenge? On who?"

"On them," Ilda shrieked, pointing at the crowd of villagers. "For years I stood in front of that classroom, trying to get knowledge into their minds, and they laughed at me, said they didn't need knowledge when they had magic. As if that weren't bad enough, they tormented and humiliated me. The only way I could make it stop was to punish them, but they still found ways. I could hear them giggling when my back was turned.

"Finally, I couldn't stand it anymore, and I burned that schoolhouse down." The witch's lips curled up in a grim smile. "When she came to me and told me about her plan to take all the magic, I knew it was my chance to finally teach this kingdom a lesson."

I marched over and grabbed Ilda's arms. "Look at me!" I said. "Who are you talking about? Who planned this?" Maybe I was a people-shaker after all.

Her wild eyes finally focused on me. "The fairies," she said. "They're the ones you want. They're the ones who took your parents."

"What? But you said you didn't know who took them."

Ilda let out a dry laugh. "I lied, just like the fairies told me to. They were behind everything. They ruined this land. And now they've ruined me."

"What about my parents?" I could barely breathe. "Are they alive?"

The witch sighed, her shoulders sagging, as if her energy had left her. "Last I heard, they were."

Blood rushed into my ears. My mom and dad were alive! "But what would the fairies want with my parents?"

"Your mother and father suspected the truth about the curse, so the fairies took them to their home base. And then they—"

Before she could say another word, a blinding flash lit up the stage and—*Poof*!—Ilda was gone.

Chapter Thirty-One

There was a stunned silence as everyone stared at the spot where Ilda had just been.

Then people in the crowd started to scream while Sir Knight rushed forward to examine the stage. All that was left of Ilda was my mother's necklace, shining in the fading sunlight.

Ilda was gone.

"Where did she go?" said Sir Knight.

"The fairies," I said, trying to process what had happened. Suddenly, I remembered the times when Ilda had mentioned that she wasn't the one making the rules, that someone would be upset if she changed the way things were done. Had she been talking about the fairies?

If the fairies really were behind my parents' disappearance, then what Ilda had said about my mom and dad literally vanishing in front of her eyes was true. And now, all these years later, they'd taken the witch too.

After I sank to the ground, I scooped up the necklace and clutched it tightly in my hand.

I still didn't know where my parents were, but at least one good thing had come of all this: I finally knew who had taken them.

● ● ●

"But why would the fairies take my land's magic?" Princess Nartha asked after I'd recounted what had happened. She, Aletha, and the old servant were the only people who hadn't been at the festival. Of course, after Aletha had heard that Ilda was gone, she'd fainted dead away, and the servant had had to carry her to her room.

"I don't know," I admitted. "But I'm going to find out."

The princess nodded and went over to her usual spot by the window. "What will we do now? All this time, I thought we simply needed to be rid of Ilda to get our magic back. But now..."

"I'm sorry," I said, wishing I could do more.

Princess Nartha let out a long sigh. "I suppose my people and I will just have to go on as we have."

"Excuse me for saying so, Your Highness, but I don't think your attitude is really helping."

She turned to me. "Excuse me?"

"If you're convinced that your kingdom can't function without magic, then it won't. But maybe if you try new things, find a way to live so that you don't need magic, your kingdom might be okay. You have to be positive, you know?"

"Be positive," she repeated. "I-I suppose you might be right. It's just that my land has always had magic. When the magic started to disappear so soon after my parents were transformed, I didn't know what to do."

I could understand feeling lost without parents, but that didn't mean the princess should just give up. "I know you can do it," I said. "You just need to have some faith in yourself."

For the first time ever, the princess actually smiled. "That is something my father used to say to me. He felt I didn't have enough faith in my ability to be a ruler one day."

Suddenly, there was a knock on the door. Then it opened and the old servant poked his head in. "Your Highness, you have visitors."

"Visitors?" she said, clearly surprised. "Who are they?"

"It's only us!" I heard Anthony say a second before he pushed past the servant and marched into the room.

Behind him were Melissa and Trish. All three of them bowed to the princess.

"What are you guys doing here?" I said.

"We thought you might need our help," said Melissa. "You know, now that the magic is really gone."

Trish stepped forward. "Your Highness," she said. "We're offering you our services."

"We might not know how to use magic," Melissa explained, "but we're really good at living without it. Heck, we've been doing it all our lives. That means we're naturals."

"For example," said Trish, pulling a teakettle from behind her back, "we're happy to show your people how to boil water without magic. It's actually pretty easy!"

I glanced at Anthony. "Was this your idea?"

He shook his head. "I wish I could take the credit, but your friends were the ones who thought of it. And the Committee even approved it after I persuaded them." He winked, and I had a feeling he'd bribed the old women with Tootsie Rolls again.

"But what about returning to your world and to your families?" said Princess Nartha. "Would you really want to stay here and help us?"

"For a little while, anyway," said Melissa. "Our parents

just think we're away on a school trip. And Anthony said he could use some magic to make sure our tests are passed and stuff." I could tell the idea of not having to study or do homework was especially appealing to her.

"It could be an exchange of information," said Trish. "We'd teach your people what we know about living normal lives, and you could teach us about your customs. Deal?"

The princess looked at me like she was asking for my approval.

I turned to my friends. "It might take a while before the villagers are okay without you." I glanced at Trish. "What about your English paper? What about the essay contest?"

Trish grinned. "Who cares about an essay when I'll have enough material to write a whole book?"

"What about you, Melissa?" I said. "Won't you miss your music?"

She shrugged. "I'll have plenty of stuff to write about while I'm here. And Sir Knight says his younger brother is a musician. He's going to introduce us. Maybe the two of us can even write a duet together." She waggled her eyebrows so enthusiastically that they looked like they might come off. Then she reached into Trish's backpack, pulled out her hockey mask, and plopped it on her head. "See? I'm ready!"

"So am I," said Trish, putting on her bike helmet. "We really want this, Jenny."

I laughed. "Then I guess it's a plan. And while you guys are here, maybe you can check on Jack once in a while. And look in on Irwin and Nessie too, and make sure they're okay without magic. You might want to leave that headgear on just in case. Or bring Sir Knight with you."

"Speaking of Sir Knight," said Trish. "I think we might have come up with a solution to his little problem. At least until we find a way to undo the curse."

"Which problem?" said Princess Nartha. "I could make a list."

"His noise pollution problem," Trish clarified. She opened the chamber door and Sir Knight strode in, totally soundlessly. He was still wearing his armor, but it was now wrapped in a layer of foam padding and duct tape.

"Now you and Princess Aletha can finally be together," Melissa said with a wistful sigh.

"If she will have me," said the knight.

"Of course I will!" said a voice from out in the hall-way. Then Aletha swept into the room and threw her arms around Sir Knight. "You're so soft and squishy!"

It was like a scene straight out of a cheesy fairy tale, which normally I would have found sickening, but I couldn't help grinning at the sight. Even though so many things still needed to be set right in this land, at least Aletha and Sir Knight could finally be happy. Even Princess Nartha looked almost pleased.

"See? My friends will be a huge help to your kingdom," I told her.

"Very well," Princess Nartha said. "With their aid, I'm sure I'll be able to make my kingdom something my parents could be proud of again." She glanced at the rug and chair in the center of the room. "I only wish I could bring them back. Do you think there's any way…?"

I bit my lip. I wanted to reassure Princess Nartha that we could change her parents back, but with Ilda gone and the magic drained, I didn't know if that was possible.

"Once I track down my parents," I said, "we'll come back here and fix everything."

The princess nodded. "Thank you for all your help, Jenny." She still looked sad, but there was genuine warmth in her voice.

"You have done our kingdom a great kindness," Aletha chimed in. Luckily, she'd forgiven me for allowing Leonard to run away. She had faith that he would find his way home eventually.

"I'm just glad your people don't hate adventurers anymore," I said. And don't blame my parents, I silently added. "Oh, and I have something for you." I rummaged around in my bag and found Ilda's first two objects. "Maybe you can burn them. It might make you feel better."

Princess Nartha glanced at the one that looked like a fly swatter. "You're giving us a carpet beater?"

I turned the object around, realizing she was right. I remembered Dr. Bradley showing me all kinds of antique objects he'd found in the basement of his new house. One of them had been for getting the dust out of carpets. That's why the object had looked so familiar.

"Why would Ilda hide this?" I said. Then I realized what a silly question that was. Ilda was insane. There didn't need to be a reason. Unless…

I glanced over at the carpet in the middle of the room, then at the rocking chair. I grabbed the spray bottle out of my bag and sniffed the contents again. This time I could place the smell: furniture polish. Of course!

I hurried over to the carpet and aimed the metal stick at it. *Thwack!*

"What are you doing?" Princess Nartha cried. "Leave

my father alone!" She tried to wrestle the handle away from me as the old servant rushed over to help her.

"Jenny-girl, are you crazy?" Anthony yelled.

"Trust me." *Thwack. Thwack. Thwack.* "I know what I'm doing."

Princess Nartha screamed and managed to yank the carpet beater out of my hand. Then she fell to her knees as if she wanted to give the carpet a hug. "Father, I'm so sorry!"

Not surprisingly, Aletha's eyes rolled back in her head and she fainted from all the commotion. Luckily, Sir Knight was there to catch her in his newly cushy arms.

The servant looked ready to throw me in the dungeon while my friends stared at me with their mouths gaping open. Before anyone could act, Princess Nartha screamed again.

"What's happening?" she said as the rug began to move on its own. It was morphing from flat and square to round and thick and person-like.

Finally, the rug finished transforming. In its place stood a stooped older man with a crooked crown on his head.

"Father?" Princess Nartha whispered.

The man was clearly confused, but his face lit up when he saw his daughter. "Nartha, dear," he said. "I'm feeling a bit peckish. Do you know if dinner is ready?"

"How…how did you do this?" Nartha asked me.

"You think that's impressive? Watch this!" I grabbed the spray bottle and spritzed the rocking chair. Almost instantly, it started to stretch and change. A few seconds later, the queen was in its place.

"Goodness," the queen said. "I have such a crick in my neck. And who are all these people?"

Princess Nartha laughed and threw her arms around both her parents, while the servant sank to his knees with tears in his eyes. Meanwhile, Sir Knight cradled the unconscious Aletha in his arms. No doubt she'd wake up, see her parents, and faint all over again. But eventually, she'd be able to share in the happiness too.

I watched the scene feeling both glad and oddly hopeful. For the first time in my life, I was sure my own parents were within my reach. They were alive. I was almost certain of it, and I was going to find them.

"I know what we need," Melissa announced, rifling around in her pocket. She pulled out a fortune, cleared her throat, and read: "'The first step to better times is to imagine them.'"

I couldn't agree more.

Chapter Thirty-Two

When I got home, I couldn't help shuddering at the sight of Aunt Evie giving her ostrich patient a therapeutic massage in the middle of the kitchen. The oversized ostrich beak brought up memories of giant birds that I knew would give me pecked-to-death nightmares for weeks.

Aunt Evie smiled when she spotted me in the doorway. Then her face changed, and I realized she was looking at the necklace around my neck. "Wasn't that your mother's?" she said. "I haven't seen that in ages. Where did you find it?"

"It's a long story." I wished more than anything that I could finally tell her the truth. And one day I would, I decided. When I found my parents and brought them back, the three of us would tell her everything, no matter what the Committee said. After all she'd been through, Aunt Evie deserved to know the whole story.

"Maybe you can tell me over dinner?" she asked. "I'm planning on making your favorite: fish casserole." She pointed to some cat food containers stacked on the counter.

"Sorry, I wish I could, but I have to go."

"When will you be home?"

I hesitated. Who knew how long I would need to track down my parents in the fairy world? It could be hours, or it could be days or even weeks. "I'm not sure," I said finally. "But I'll be back as soon as I can. I promise."

I hurried out the door and around the corner to Dr. Bradley's house. I expected to find the doctor rummaging through piles of trash like usual, but instead he and Anthony were sitting in the living room with somber looks on their faces. Those looks were a far cry from the big grin that had been spread across Anthony's face when he'd dropped me off at home only minutes earlier.

"What's wrong?" I said.

"You disobeyed the Committee," the doctor said. "And you tricked Anthony into helping you." For the first time I could remember, he sounded upset with me.

I swallowed. "But it worked out in the end, didn't it? I got rid of Ilda and saved the king and queen. Wasn't it worth the risk?"

"The Committee members don't see it that way," said Dr. Bradley. "They are furious with you."

"What else is new? I've decided to stop caring about hurting the Committee's feelings. It's not worth the stress."

"This is serious, Jenny-girl," said Anthony. "Dr. Bradley said they're talking about kicking you out all together, stripping your adventurer title."

Yes, I'd disobeyed the Committee members, but only so I could follow my adventurer instincts. How could they not understand that? "You talked them out of it, right?"

Dr. Bradley sighed. "They've agreed to let you stay on for now, but you're on probation. One more misstep and—"

"Okay, I get it. I'm sorry. I won't do anything like that again. I can't believe we're even talking about this when I finally have a lead on what happened to my parents. Ilda said they were taken by the fairies to their home base, wherever that is."

"Fairy Land," Dr. Bradley said with a thoughtful nod.

"Fairy Land?" I repeated. "That's even worse than Merland. It sounds like an amusement park, not a place where evil fairies live." I expected Dr. Bradley to at least crack a smile, but his face stayed somber. "Why aren't you more excited about this? My parents are alive! We know who took them. This is the lead we've been waiting for."

"The problem, Jenny," said Dr. Bradley, "is that I'm afraid the Committee members won't allow you to go."

I gawked at him. "What are you talking about?"

"They believe it's too dangerous."

"So, they just want to let my parents rot in Fairy Land?"

"Of course not," said Dr. Bradley. "But perhaps the Committee is right to be cautious. What if the witch was lying? What if your parents weren't taken by the fairies?"

"Ilda had no reason to lie! The fairies stole her magic and betrayed her. And they tried to silence her when she started to tell me the truth."

"I'm afraid the Committee has already made up its mind." Dr. Bradley shook his head slowly. "The members feel they can't allow you to go into a land we know so little about."

My blood felt like lava in my veins. "So that's it then? Case closed?"

"They'll study the matter further," he said. "Maybe one day they'll know enough to be able to put a plan into action."

"One day?" I said. "I've been waiting seven years. My *parents* have been waiting seven years! Don't they care about that?"

"Of course they do, Jenny-girl," Anthony jumped in.

"But they also care about you. We all do. Do you really want to rush into danger when you don't even know what's waiting for you?"

"Isn't that what I always do? Isn't that what being an adventurer is all about?" As I said it, I realized Jasmine would probably disagree with me. To her, being an adventurer was a job, but for me it was my life. And finding my parents was so much more than just another adventure. It was one mission I could never give up on.

"Sorry," I added. "There's nothing the Committee members can do to convince me. I'm going after my parents, with or without their help."

Dr. Bradley let out another long sigh. "I was afraid you would say that."

"Jenny-girl, think about this for a second," said Anthony. "They'll fire you. You won't be an adventurer anymore."

I should have felt shocked or hurt or angry at the thought, but I just felt nothing. The truth was that if being an adventurer was going to stop me from getting my parents back, then it was no good for me anyway.

"Then they'll fire me," I said flatly.

Silence buzzed through the room, wrapping around all three of us.

"Are you really sure this is what you want?" Anthony finally asked.

"No," I admitted, sinking into an armchair. "But if the Committee members are willing to give up on my parents so easily, then I don't want to work for them."

"So what are you going to do?" said Anthony.

"Go to Fairy Land."

The gnome shook his head and chomped into a cucumber. I had to admit, he was starting to look a little leaner. "That's it, Jenny-girl?" he said. "That's your whole plan?"

I couldn't blame him for staring at me like I'd completely lost my mind. Maybe I had.

"How will you get there?" said Dr. Bradley.

"I-I don't know," I admitted, realizing that yet again I was charging into things without thinking them through. In truth, I had no idea where Fairy Land was. And since I had no magical abilities, I had no way to get there on my own. Unless I could steal a spaceship or something. "I don't suppose either of you would be willing to help me?"

Anthony and Dr. Bradley looked at each other. I watched another one of their silent, head-nodding conversations. No doubt they were working out a way to lock me up in a mental institution.

Finally, they turned back to me.

"Of course we'll help you," said Dr. Bradley.

"Really? But what about the Committee?" I turned to Anthony. "What about your reunion? We probably won't be back in time. All that dieting will be for nothing."

"Don't even worry about that, Jenny-girl. Bottom line is that we agree with you. The Committee is being dumb about this whole thing." He shrugged. "Besides, I've realized I kind of like health food." He bit off another hunk of cucumber, and for once, he didn't even cringe.

"We loved your parents," Dr. Bradley added. "If there's any way to get them back, we must at least try. Even if the Committee doesn't approve."

I rushed over and threw my arms around Anthony. Then around Dr. Bradley. "Thank you! Thank you, thank you, thank you!"

Dr. Bradley let out a sad chuckle. "Don't thank us yet. We can take you to Fairy Land, but I'm afraid we might not be much help. The Committee was right about some things. We know very little about the fairies."

"We'll figure it out. We always do. I promise you won't regret this." I ran my fingers over my mother's necklace and then glanced down at my bracelet, which I had decided to

214

wear again. Both pieces of jewelry seemed to be humming with excitement, just like I was. My parents had never felt so within my reach. "When do we leave?" I asked.

Anthony shrugged. "How about now?"

I couldn't believe it. After all these years, this could finally be my chance to get my family back. I smiled. "Now would be perfect."

Acknowledgments

We have to do the cheesy thank-you stuff again? Ugh, Jenny would *not* approve. Luckily, she's away on an adventure right now, so here we go.

To Ray Brierly for being the bestest husband ever and for not being afraid to tell me if my silly jokes aren't funny.

To my family and friends for always rooting for me and for forcing my debut novel into the hands of anyone who can read.

To my writing partners and cheerleaders—especially Megan Kudrolli, Alisa Libby, Heather Kelly, and Sarah Chessman—for unlimited brainstorming help and occasional therapy sessions.

To Ammi-Joan Paquette, agent extraordinaire, for being just plain awesome.

To Aubrey Poole and the rest of the fantastic

Sourcebooks folks for giving me the opportunity to send Jenny on more adventures.

And to the fans of *My Very UnFairy Tale Life* who have blown me away with their enthusiasm and support. You rock!

About the Author

Born in Poland and raised in the United States, Anna Staniszewski grew up loving stories (especially fairy tales) in both Polish and English. After studying theater at Sarah Lawrence College, she attended the Center for the Study of Children's Literature at Simmons College. She

Sedman Photography

was named the 2006–2007 Writer-in-Residence at the Boston Public Library and a winner of the 2009 PEN New England Susan P. Bloom Discovery Award. Currently, Anna lives outside Boston with her husband and their adorably crazy dog, Emma. When she's not writing, Anna spends her time teaching, reading, and jumping rope with mermaids. You can visit her at www.annastan.com.